WRITING
BACK

Published in the UK in 2022 by Cork House Publishing

Copyright 2022 George Corbett

George Corbett has asserted their right under
the Copyright, Designs and Patents Act, 1988,
to be identified as the author of this work.

This book is a work of fiction, and except in the case of
historical or geographical fact, any resemblance to names,
place and characters, living or dead, is purely coincidental.

Paperback ISBN 978-1-7397404-0-5
Hardback ISBN 978-1-7397404-2-9
eBook ISBN 978-1-7397404-1-2

Cover design and typeset by SpiffingCovers

A COLLECTION
OF SHORT STORIES
OF AN ADULT NATURE

WRITING
BACK

*Stories from
the brink*

GEORGE CORBETT

CONTENTS

Doppelgänger

"Be yourself; everyone else is already taken."

-Oscar Wilde

CHAPTER 1

Excuse me, please could I be you?

Our hero, or villain depending on how you look at it, is a pretty weird guy. His name is Trevor Langdon, although not for long. The thing with Trevor, is that Trevor has grown somewhat bored of being Trevor. In fact, he dislikes it so much, that Trevor went on the look out for a new life - a possibility most of us have considered at some point.

Trevor's search began, and also ended, in Coconut Grove - a fairly chilled area of South Miami - equipped with a thriving nightlife, beach views, and the main thing that Trevor was looking for - his doppelgänger

Trevor had a few 'rules' for his new life. The man he chose could not be married or in a relationship - mainly because he did not consider surgery on his member a viable possibility. He would prefer that they were unemployed, as he did not really fancy taking on a job he did not understand. Ideally, they would be rich. Finally, the person needed to be social - but not to social. A vague parameter - but important. After all, any friends he would inherit would no doubt have histories with his new identity - a difficult hurdle to overcome. But not impossible.

Trevor wished that his new life could come with a small handbook detailing the person's history, but this was in fact where he drew the line of ridiculous.

Trevor made the move to Miami in February of 2020. He rented a small apartment in Coral Gables - also in South Miami. The final straw had been his sacking from his job in Tampa - a number of customers lodged complaints with Pizza City that their deliveries were, on occasion, mysteriously missing a few slices. Trevor, of course, denied any wrongdoing, but the tomato sauce on his chin proved to be his undoing.

Trevor spent the next few weeks formulating his masterplan before packing up a few possessions, including a DVD of Basic Instinct (He rather liked Sharon Stone), his burgundy dressing gown, and his favourite Playboy magazine (the less said about that combination, the better).

His new apartment was, for want of a better combination of words, a shit hole. But Trevor did not care, he would not be here for long. He did draw the line at the mouldy piece of bread he found in the shower of all places, but he could not yet afford a cleaner, so he pegged his nose and picked it up using one of his three t shirts. It had a print of The Ramones on it, whom he did not much care for, so it joined the furry slice in the trash outside. Trevor wondered what music he would like in his new life.

Trevor's search was, initially, fairly unrewarding. He thought of himself as a fairly generic looking human - he had short, cropped brown hair, white skin tanned in the Florida sun, a stubble and brown eyes. He was not overweight, but also not too skinny. The job at Pizza City had helped. He felt his look was also changeable, depending on the person that he set his sights on. He understood that humans were not chameleons, but in the sunshine state, a bit of nip and tuck was not uncommon. If anything, it was strangely encouraged.

It was on a suitably warm night in June that Trevor caught sight of a potential doppelgänger. Trevor had been at an Irish bar called Mandy's, minding his own business whilst also nursing a pint of Guinness. he was careful not to get drunk, in case he saw someone he thought looked like him, when in fact they looked nothing like him. A rather odd variation of Beer goggles, you might say.

It had been one of the fellow patrons, bizarrely, that had pointed him out. A man who looked very similar to Trevor had approached the bar with a smooth swagger that Trevor would have to work on, and one of the patrons sitting near to Trevor had been the one to drunkenly point it out, rather pleased with himself, that they looked like twins. Trevor, who had not immediately noticed the man - could not believe his luck. The patron probably did not realise the sentence that he had just handed to Trevor's 'twin.'

Trevor said nothing at the time, and the man at the bar who had been accused of being his lookalike looked a bit awkward, before smiling and turning away with his beer. The man was drinking with two other men - which earned him his first tick on Trevor's mental check list.

Trevor followed him home that night, to Coconut Grove, and this is where he earned his second and third ticks. The man's apartment was in fact a house - a detached house. Initially, Trevor thought that this would mean he had family, but the man appeared to live on his own. Trevor had spent the night, and many days and nights afterwards, watching him through the window. The house was sparsely decorated, with the pictures on the wall mainly being movie posters, films like Pulp Fiction and Die Hard, and on one wall sat a dart board. The man seemed to live off takeaways, and spent his weekends cheering on the Florida Gators - the local American Football team - on his ludicrously oversized TV. To all intensive purposes, it was a bachelor pad. Perfect.

Women occasionally came and went, which excited Trevor. It did not appear that the man paid for them - and Trevor hoped he might have the same luck. One night, Trevor had watched the man throw his SIM card away and replace it with another, but Trevor thought nothing of it. The man had a dog, a big dog, and Trevor did not like dogs, but he could learn to like them, he supposed. This was the man.

Trevor formulated a plan. He did not want to kill the man, as he might potentially need him for information on his history. He decided the best place to keep him would be his apartment, until he was ready to dispose of him.

What's more, Trevor did not think he would need any surgery. Trevor did not like hospitals, and imagined doctors would likely be suspicious of a man who had suddenly, for instance, changed blood groups.

Florida being a state which allowed the carrying of a concealed weapon, Trevor purchased a firearm with the last of his meagre savings - a Ruger 57, at The Home Depot . Trevor enjoyed the slogan 'fun to shoot, cool to own,' God bless America. Trevor did hope, however, that he would not actually have to fire it. He couldn't afford a silencer, and was not a particularly good shot.

The night Trevor decided to kidnap the man - he drove to his home in his rather rusty Lexus LS 400 - excited about the shimmering BMW in the man's drive. He knocked on the door, then drew his weapon to the startled man. The man had asked if Trevor was with the police, which Trevor scoffed at. Trevor led the man to the Lexus, and drove him back to the apartment. He handcuffed him to the basin in the bathroom. A brisk check of the man showed that he had no tattoos or birthmarks - it was almost becoming too good to be true. The man was very quiet, almost accepting of his fate, which Trevor found strange.

Indeed, the only thing the man had asked was, "Is this about Freddie Watts." Trevor merely shook his head, before taking his wallet, keys and phone and leaving the apartment.

Trevor checked the ID card. It was incredible how similar they both looked.

Trevor was now no longer Trevor, he had a new name.

Richard Conway

Trevor had done it.....

CHAPTER 2

Hi, I'm Richard.

It's probably worth pointing out that before Trevor left the real Richard to rot in his dirty bathroom, he had done the decent thing and explained to him what he was doing. Richard had not seemed too bothered about Trevor taking his identity, and had even gone to the trouble of pointing out his favourite drinking spots. He had, however, asked Trevor if he could therefore assume Trevor's identity for whatever little time remained of his life. Trevor happily obliged, leaving Richard with his ID card and birth certificate.

The real Richard, or Rich, as he pointed out most people called him - would remain chained up in the bathroom. Trevor did promise to come back and feed him most days, or to collect passwords or background history. He quickly forgot about Rich's strange request to be Trevor. Trevor did not think anyone would ever want to be him, especially if they were chained up in a bathroom.

Trevor left his Lexus outside his apartment, and used the money in Rich's wallet to take a taxi to his new home. Living the high life already, he thought. He had already got Rich's PIN number for his credit card and the password for his Iphone. Trevor stopped the taxi to check the balance of his account. His eyes almost popped out of the socket when the screen showed him that he was now the proud owner of over two million US dollars. He withdrew two thousand. He would tip the taxi driver, he thought.

Suddenly, Miami looked entirely different to him - he had a wealth of possibilities. Trevor's strange little brain was working in overdrive when thinking about all the things he could do, he could do anything with that money. Hell, he could jump out of a fucking plane with Sharon Stone strapped to his back if he really wanted! Trevor did, however, want to impose boundaries on himself. He felt he would arouse suspicion if he lived a life too far different from the one Rich had been living. From what Trevor had watched, Rich only went out to drink in the evenings, occasionally with a few friends, but mainly to bring home girls - which Trevor, of course, had no problem with. Trevor, decided, that he would try and avoid the friends, and stick with the women.

His first night at the apartment was glorious. Rich had a rather large set of Bluetooth speakers, and Trevor was pleased to discover a Spotify account on his phone. Trevor deleted Rich's old playlist - wondering who on earth Oasis and The Stone Roses were. Trevor did not know what Brit-pop was, and did not wish to learn. Instead, he cranked up his favourite artist Kanye West. Trevor thought the dog was judging him for this, doesn't everyone love Kanye West, Trevor thought?

The dog, which Trevor discovered after a bit of research, was a black and white border collie. Trevor later discovered his name was Vincent. Trevor did not ask if that was after Vincent Vega, who of course sat staring at him from the Pulp Fiction poster on his new wall.

As Trevor went through Rich's rather overgrown wardrobe, Vincent sat and watched suspiciously. Trevor did not worry if the dog was the only one that knew his secret, and to be honest Trevor enjoyed the company, even if Vincent did not.

Trevor marvelled at his new clothes - pristinely clean white shirts, expensive Hugo Boss blazers and Diesel jeans. Trevor even occasionally wore Rich's Gators top, which had his new surname, Conway, on the back. He would wear it and watch the matches, even though he did not understand the rules. Nothing like getting into character.

Trevor went out on the town on his second night, hoping that if he splashed the cash, he would get the girls. He had perfected his look based on a couple of photos Rich had in his camera roll. He had shaved off his rather pathetic stubble, used the expensive skin cream that sat in the bathroom, and dressed himself to impress. He gawped at himself in the mirror, impressed with his transformation into a high flyer.

Trevor came home that night with a woman on his arm, and he had never felt better. She was clearly impressed with his home - which was exactly what he wanted. She had even told him that he smelt good. No one had ever told Trevor that he smelt good. He had allowed himself to drink more now that he did not have to worry about finding a suitable match for himself - he thought it had been the booze that had allowed him to talk to woman, but it most likely was the cash that he flashed in the bar. Either way, Trevor did not care. He had not had sex in years. The women, generally, left his home unsatisfied. Trevor, on the other hand, could not have been happier.

Trevor still returned to see his cap-tee - who still, strangely, was not complaining. Trevor almost wanted the man to moan - why on earth was he so willingly having his life taken away from him. Trevor did not want to kill him until the man displayed some sort of problem with Trevor stealing his life. It almost seemed like Rich wanted Trevor to be him.

Regardless of this strange anomaly, Trevor carried on making the most of his new life. He drove around Miami with the roof down on his convertible, Chris Brown and Pitbull reverberating out of the new state of the art Pioneer radio he had quickly got installed. People would often look at him strangely for this, Trevor could not understand why. One man even shouted woman beater at him. Bizarre.

By night, Trevor continued to traverse the various bars and clubs of Coconut Grove and the surrounding areas. He picked up woman, and avoided any texts or phone calls that appeared to be an invite to meet friends. He did not need Rich's friends. One night one of them approached him, Trevor did not catch his name, and told him he looked a little unwell. Trevor quickly found a way out of the conversation, and decided to buy some Gym Equipment. One session proved enough for Trevor to decide he didn't need to be muscly to get women.

One beautifully sunny morning, when Trevor had shepherded his latest conquest, (who certainly did not look as good as he remembered, regularly went to the toilet, and appeared to have a problem with her nose) out of the door, he reclined on his sofa and flicked on the television.

It was the news - which Trevor tended to avoid, but he was hungover and couldn't be bothered to flick through the channels. Besides, there had been a murder, and Trevor quite enjoyed a juicy murder.

"Police where called to the home of Freddie Watts, who lives in South Beach. His body had been discovered by his landlady - Victoria Sparks - after she noticed he had not left for several weeks. Mr Watts had two gunshot wounds to the head. The police ask anyone with any information to come forward.."

Trevor's brain was rather muddled, but he could have sworn that he recognised the name Freddie Watts. Trevor decided that it was nothing, and flicked over to the music channel, excited that they were showing Nicki Minaj's latest song.

CHAPTER 3

Richard Conway, the amateur murderer

At this point it might have been wise for Trevor to have talked to his prisoner, who was no doubt feeling a little smug right now. A feeling that not many prisoners, in the long history of cap-tees, have ever felt.

The name Freddie Watts, was, after all, one of only a number of things that Rich had said to him during their brief interactions. Trevor's mind had, unfortunately, become too full of what he considered to be the finer things in life - the bottom of an overpriced bottle of vodka, expensive clothes which became a little bit tighter every day, and inebriated young ladies with under cover powder problems.

The next thing on Trevor's rather self indulgent bucket list was a holiday. In his previous life, which Trevor begrudgingly had to think about every now and again, he had never left the USA. He was disappointed to discover that he did not own a private jet - but rather more cheerful when he realised it was easy enough to charter one. The next question was his destination - Trevor knew little of the world outside the American borders apart from what he had seen in movies. He liked the idea of being the millionaire playboy in Italy from The Talented Mr Ripley - although he rather hoped Matt Damon would not come and 'rescue' him.

Trevor did not want the leave Rich though - he had grown strangely fond of his prisoner, and Trevor was many things, but he was not a killer. He knew that he could not release him, and that if he left him for an extended period of time - Rich would probably die. Trevor did not want Rich to die. Because if Rich dies, and his body is discovered, then Trevor would have to go back to being Trevor. Trevor did not want to be Trevor ever again, besides, Rich seemed to quite enjoy being Trevor. So, in Trevor's eyes - everyones a winner.

So, for the time being, Trevor shelved his plans to go on holiday. It proved to be a poor decision, like many of Trevor's decisions, as at least he would have been out of the country when a rather startling discovery was made in the forensic section of the Miami PD - which is where our story will now take us.

*

Inspector Ramirez and Bryce Thompson, the Miami PD coroner and resident funny man, stood over the corpse of Freddie Watts. His body was now sheet white, apart from the rather mangled forehead which had two holes in it. These holes had, fairly recently been the home of two 9mm rounds from a Glock 47.

The investigation had not been a particularly difficult one for Inspector Ramirez. In fact, he was now sure that he had his man - he just had a rather strange habit of looking at the corpse one more time and informing it he was about to make an arrest. He liked to think of it as giving the dead, decaying body a sense of closure. We all have the things that make us tick, after all.

Freddie Watts, in the murky underworld of Miami, had a price on his head. Apparently, the price had been about two million dollars. He had developed a rather dangerous habit of stealing money, but breaking into a chain of jewellery stores owned by a kingpin known only as The Bull had proved rather silly. It had, in fact, cost him his life.

Inspector Ramirez's investigation, though initially slow, as The Bull had seemingly vanished - took a bit of a turn when he discovered that a man called Richard Conway, who had been a childhood friend of The Bull's lovely wife, Christina (also disappeared), had recently had his various money troubles miraculously resolved. The failed stock broker's bank account had recently been injected with a cool two million from a rather vague company called SMART Energy. A quick google search proved that this company did not exist. This rather aroused Inspector Ramirez' s interest in the man.

Inspector Ramirez was a little disappointed to discover that his suspect was actually a very poor excuse for a murderer. He had recently bought a Glock 47 from a gun store called Shoot Straight, which was about two kilometres from his home, and he had also been caught on CCTV close to Watts' house around the time the coroner deemed the killing must have taken place. He didn't even wear a cap or a wooly hat. An amateur - the inspector thought. He preferred a bit more of a challenge.

Inspector Ramirez had also spoken to a couple of Mr Conway's friends; one in particular - a bulky, curly haired man with suspiciously red eyes and a rather large appetite - called Matt, had said that he had seen Rich fairly recently - but Rich had not looked himself and had found a way to escape the conversation particularly hastily, which was, apparently, unlike him. Matt, and the other friends the Inspector spoke too, whose names he could not recall, had all said that Rich no longer answered their calls, but they had caught sight of him at bars, usually mixing with the opposite sex. They said it was strange for them to be alienated from him in such a way, but Ramirez suspected that Rich probably worried about acting oddly after committing such a heinous crime.

What the Inspector did find rather bizarre, however, was Mr Conways' more recent activities. When one murders another human being for money, one tends to flee the country, or at least lay low for a little while. Mr Conway appeared to have done the opposite. He had a brief period where he had stayed home except when he ventured out to the occasional bar, but more recently he had really been splashing the cash.

A short investigation into Mr Conways' rather volatile bank account showed transactions at various bars more or less every night - alongside a recent splurge in the Bay Harbour district of Miami. Bal Habour played host to some of the cities most expensive designer stores - Gucci, Versace, Georgio Armani etc.

On top of that, Mr Conway made regular trips to the DVD shop (had he not heard of Netflix?!) and to Dirty Dawgs. A local pet shop.

Inspector Ramirez thought it odd that a man who had just committed a cold blooded killing could enjoy himself so much, perhaps this self indulgence helped to take his mind of the crimes he has just committed - however, if Inspector Ramirez had been the killer, the first thing he probably would have done, would be to have left the country.

The problem was Mr Conway was, in fact, not Mr Conway. Mr Conway was a pizza delivery boy from Tampa called Trevor, who had no idea that he had just committed a first degree murder, and that a warrant had just been issued for his arrest.

CHAPTER 4

Maybe this was not such a great idea after all

So now, naturally, things start to get a little bit spicy. Whilst Mr Ramirez waved goodbye to the deceased thief - Trevor had been out taking Vincent for a walk. It had taken him a surprisingly long time to work out that this is how you avoid the dog shitting on the floor. Plus, he thought the exercise might do him some good. The expensive food and steady flow of beer were causing his belts to be a little tight. The regular sex, apparently, was not proving to be enough exercise.

Whilst Trevor took in the fresh Miami air, Vincent trotting along beside him, still rather confused about the new scent of his owner, Inspector Ramirez and two armed police officers arrived at Rich's front door. After a particularly loud knock, Ramirez gave the all clear to the men to break down the door - an order to which they seemed rather excited about. They had not yet had an opportunity to use the new 'Hydraulic door blaster.' Boys and their toys.

The Door Blaster was a bit of anti climax, simply exerting pressure on the lock and popping it through, a silent affair - which of course made a lot more sense, however it was hardly the exhilarating spectacle of battering a door off its hinges. Anyhow, they were in. They quickly ascertained that Mr Conway was out.

Trevor was coming round the corner just as the police left the house, and it is very possible that he might have pee'd just a little bit when he saw the two police cars outside his new home and the door open. Police do not break in unless it's serious. Very serious.

Trevor knew he had to get away, he could suddenly feel his beautiful new life slipping away. Something he was also not at all good at. The bonus was that they did not know that he was there. What Trevor decided to do was the latest in a long line of terrible decisions. He dropped Vincent's lead and bolted, instantly knocking over an unsuspecting child who had stood close to him to watch the rather exciting scene unfolding over the road. Trevor went down with the child, swearing and cursing as he fell on top of the acne covered hero.

Vincent then decided to get involved the only way he knew how - to bark, relentlessly, drawing just about as much attention to his new owner he possibly could. Naturally, this alerted the policeman, and their disappointment at the Door Blaster quickly gave way to another surge of excitement. Trevor attempted to get up, but he was not fast enough - and it was not long before the boy realised that Trevor was the man the police were after, and attached himself to Trevor's leg. Inspector Ramirez would recall that particular image with some amusement.

He was quickly handcuffed and read his Miranda rights, before being placed in the back of the police car. When Ramirez mentioned the name Freddie Watts, Trevor quickly remembered where he had heard it before, and now fully understood exactly why Rich had been so happy to remain chained up. A perpetually irritating moment of irritation dawned in his brain. Swear words followed.

Trevor was now ready to go back to his old life - he did not believe he would do well in prison. He even, dare I say it, felt a pang of regret.

Inspector Ramirez, naturally, thought that was that. He even tried to run - if they try to run, they were usually guilty. All the evidence stacked up against him, and they probably wouldn't even need to find the murder weapon - what a luxury!

Trevor knew he would have to tell the truth - he would either go down for kidnapping or murder, and of course kidnapping looked like a much more lucrative ticket at this point. So he came clean to the Inspector - who quite clearly was not expecting such a ridiculous story. The Inspector merely stared at him blankly, before deciding to excuse himself for a cigarette, to mull things over.

Trevor hoped that handing over his home address would be the clincher. Ramirez would go over to his apartment, extract Rich from the basin, and then he would be home free. Well, after he had dealt with consequences of trying to steal someones life - but that seemed fairly menial at this point, in the grand scheme of things.

So Ramirez got his squad together - this time he had the apartment keys and would not need the aid of the Hydraulic Door Blaster - and they headed over to Trevor's apartment. Sure enough, in the bathroom they found Rich. He did not look to hot, but the man was alive. He did not, however, look like much of a murderer. Not that killers tend to have a particular look.

When Ramirez asked Rich who he was - of course, everyone thought that he would also claim to be Trevor as well, I mean no one would want to be Rich, after all, he was the killer! Immediately he was arrested - but little did we know, Rich had had plenty of time to formulate a rather interesting tale of his own.

Rich's story is as follows - Trevor had stalked Rich having found out about the bounty on Freddie Watts' head. He had chained up Rich, then carried out the killing himself. Then claimed to be Rich, collected the bounty, and carried on living Rich's life. Trevor was planning to switch the men back and then make off with the money, but it became apparent that he rather took to his new life.

Now what evidence could there possibly be for this, well this is the interesting bit. Of course, there was CCTV of Trevor at the bar the night he first met Rich, Furthermore, a neighbours camera saw Trevor heading back and forth from Rich's house when Trevor had first started watching him. Of course, the one thing that Trevor, the real Trevor, did not know - was that the night that Rich committed the killing was the night before he decided to take him, the night he had seen him switch the SIM card in his phone. A horrible coincidence, but it also meant that Rich's story now matched perfectly with this timeline.

Whats more, is that Rich knew that the police had not found the murder weapon. How could they - it was the one thing that he had done sensibly. He had disposed of it in a scrap yard - and watched the car get physically destroyed, the next morning. Also, even though Rich had rather stupidly not concealed his identity the night of the murder, he had managed to wear a pair of gloves. Therefore, there was absolutely no forensic evidence.

What it came down to now, was Rich's word against Trevor.

And this is where our story comes to an end. Of course, we know the real story. The poor jury of that trial, however, did not. It was impossible to tell who was telling the truth.

It came to an end that was just bizarre as the story as itself. Inspector Ramirez decided to bring a third party into the court room - and it proved to be an inspired decision. So in came Vincent, accompanied by a handler, and both Rich and Trevor were ordered to call the dog.

Of course, Vincent went towards Rich, the real Rich.

A Christmas Miracle at Evesham Hall

"The way I see it, having a paranormal encounter like seeing a ghost is kind of like winning the creepiest lottery imaginable"

- David Godwin

PART 1

Evesham Hall

The taxi passed through the creaky gates of Evesham Hall. The long, windy drive was covered with a bed of untouched bright white snow. A huge frozen lake curled around a deserted maintenance shed in the distance. The unwelcoming trees whispered between themselves, preparing for the first occupant in over 16 years.

Rachael peered out the taxi window, astonished that she had no memory of this place. She watched the huge building appear through the falling snow, dark and menacing in the distance. Rachael knew one thing - this Christmas she would be alone.

More alone than ever.

We are sorry to have to tell you, Miss Bristol, that your father has left your home in France and most of his assets to his mistress.
He did, however, many years ago opened a trust account in your name, which you have access to. Your father has also left you the deeds to your childhood home, Evesham Hall.

Rachael shivered as she thought of France. Her father's retirement had allowed her family to uproot from Evesham hall and move there when she was just 3 years old - which would probably explain why she had no memory of this monstrous building in front of her. She always thought that he had sold the place.

When her mother died 5 years ago, her father had been broken, tarnished with grief and misery. After a year or so, he had taken a new lover, a stiff, cold French woman called Claudette, who had slowly poisoned her father against Rachael.

When her father finally died, Claudette had got what she wanted - most of her father's money and their home in France.

Her life had been total isolation - she had never had a boyfriend, and had been home schooled in France, the language barriers had meant her only friend had been her father's Yorkshire terrier - Dex, who sadly had passed away two years ago, making her last two years in France a living hell. She was terrified of people, and uncomfortable in her own skin.

The taxi came to a halt outside the rickety front door - the years had been hard on the exterior of this place. She had been told that kids from the local town had attempted to loot the place over the years, a couple of the windows were boarded up, whilst a large shiny new lock on the front door looked horribly out of place on the stained brown oak.

Rachael waved goodbye to the grunting taxi driver, who had clearly judged her for her apparent wealth. The lock clicked as she turned the key, and she eased open the door and entered the building.

The howling wind bellowed through the dark entrance hall. She flicked on the light, illuminating the cold environment in front of her. As she wandered around the various rooms on the ground floor, most of which contained old furniture covered with dusty sheets, she began to feel smaller and smaller. She would get this place on the market as soon as possible, the repairs were monumental, and this was no place for a single young girl.

Her first night at Evesham Hall had been sleepless. The heating had coughed and spluttered all night, barely keeping the cold air from outside at bay. She had slept in a dressing gown in the huge master bedroom, her few possessions at the foot of the bed. She felt like a needle lost in a forgotten haystack.

She made her way down to the kitchen, most of the appliances old and mouldy, and the fridge bare. She sighed, knowing she would need to go into the town, and pottered upstairs to get changed.

Rachel stared at herself in the mirror. Whilst she did not know it, Rachael was an understated beauty. Her pale skin complimented her golden blonde hair. Her watery blue eyes hiding the anguish that lay beneath them. She was tall, and her love of swimming had allowed her to develop a stunning figure that Claudette had secretly been enormously jealous of, fuelling her hatred and bullying of Rachael.

As she wrapped her enormous warm coat around her body, she froze as she heard the soft crying of a child. It was coming from one of the many guest rooms. Terrified, Rachael debated running - but what struck her was the vulnerability of the tears. They reminded her of her own tears in France.

She tiptoed out into the corridor and followed the sound of the crying, the floorboards creaking beneath her, the fear etched all over her pale face. She found the door which contained the source of the sound, and pushed it open.

PART 2

Isabella

Rachael went to scream, but nothing came out. The small figure on the end of the bed swivelled and looked at her. It was a little girl.

The girl's yellowy eyes looked up at Rachael, her skin the colour of the snow falling in the window, tears streaking her tiny cheeks.

"H-hello?' Spluttered Rachael, completely entranced by what was in front of her. The girl stared at her, and the crying turned to sniffling, and then subsided completely.

"Hello, have you seen my mummy?" Asked the little girl, pointing to an old dusty oil painting that was on the wall. The other pictures around the house had been taken down or covered up, but this one was clean, and hung majestically in the middle of the bedroom wall. "It's Christmas soon, and I want to tell her that I lost Snowball, maybe she can help me find her."

Stunned, Rachael walked over to the painting. A family stood in front of Evesham Hall, the setting completely different. The painting oozed warmth, the family in it happy and full of life. The little girl stood in front of her parents, her long chestnut brown hair blowing in the gentle breeze, clutching a little stuffed white rabbit. The hall itself looked beautiful and clean, a world away from the state it was in now. In the bottom corner was a signature and a date - 1908. Over a hundred years ago.

The little girl pushed off the bed and came and stood next to Rachael, the tears completely stopped now. Her little hand reached out and held onto the bottom of Rachael's coat, Rachael was entranced by her.

Feeling a bit more at ease, and overcome with empathy for the girl Rachael held her hand in hers, it was frozen cold, she had never felt anything like it. "Whats your name, little one," Rachael asked. "My names Isabella, but my mummy and daddy call me Bel. Are you an angel, you look like an angel," the girl said inquisituvely

Rachael laughed, it had been a long time since anyone had given her a compliment. She instantly liked Isabella, remembering her own isolated childhood, longing for her mother to come back, to make everything better.

"I live here now Bel, I'm afraid I don't know where your mummy is, but I can certainly have a look for her. In the mean time, how about I be your friend? I don't really have any friends and this place is very new to me. Could you show me around? We can also have a look for Snowball, is that your rabbit by any chance?"

Isabella smiled, the gaps in her teeth and sudden excitement all emphasising her endearing childlike nature. The two of them spent the rest of the morning wandering around the enormous house, Isabella regaling tales in every room of her mummy and daddy, all the fun she had had. Rachael was enjoying her company, the isolation seeping away. She had instantly connected with Isabella, and wanted to help this girl however she could.

"Im sorry Bel, but the fridge is empty and I must go into town to get some food before night time! I don't really know my way so I do not want to get lost." Bel looked scared, no doubt afraid to lose the first human contact she had in what must be many many years. Gauging the situation, Rachael took off her watch. "How about I leave you with this - it was my Mummys and its very expensive. I would not go anywhere without it, so if you have it then you will know I will come back. I will try and get some Christmas decorations as well, and we can put them up together."

Isabella gave a big toothy grin and nodded, skipping off out of the kitchen into the corridor. Rachael peered around the corner of the doorway to see that the girl had vanished into the cold air of the house, and the silence returned once more.

PART 3

Evesham

The walk into town had taken longer than expected, the deep snow locking her furry boots in and stopping her from walking at speed. Rachael had a lot on her mind. She wanted to go to the library to find out what she could about the history of the Hall, she also needed food and decorations. One more stop had been added to her mental list - a toyshop.

As she approached the town, it was buzzing with activity. It was Christmas Eve and the shoppers were rushing around getting in their last minute shopping. Rachael had loved Christmas as a child when her mother had been around. The house had been full of lavish decorations, a huge tree, and the Christmas lunch around the turkey had always bought many smiles and laughter. Memories she would cherish forever.

Claudette had ruined that, always making her father take her away for a lavish holiday over the festive season, leaving Rachael stuck with a carer who spoke barely any English. No decorations went up, and she didn't even get a present until they returned, usually a meaningless trinket from wherever their travels had taken them.

She was determined to make this year different now that she had met Isabella, she had someone to look after, someone to make an effort for. Just like her mother had always made an effort for her.

She walked past some carol singers, joyously performing *Silent Night,* dropping a few coins into their hat. She was growing to like her new town immediately, it was cosy, the people smiled at her as she walked past. Perhaps it was just the Christmas cheer. Either way, she already felt more comfortable than she had in a long time.

Rachael entered the library, a small building, looking a bit naked alongside the hustle and bustle of the local pub, *The White Horse*. The elderly, curly haired woman at the desk looked up and smiled as she entered.

"Hello love, you must be new here! Good with faces I am, How can I help you?" She asked merrily.

"Good afternoon, I'm Rachael, I've just moved into the area. I was wondering if you had any history on Evesham Hall. I've just moved in there, and I wanted to know more about it."

The woman looked her up and down. "My god, your Richards's daughter! Rachael, yes that was it! Great man he was, shocked we all were when he just upped and left. I hope you get that place back to it's glory days. In the far corner my love, do you need me to show you?"

Rachael shook her head, and made her way to the history section wondering just how popular her father had been in the village. She quickly found the book she was looking for; *A History of Evesham Hall*. It was dated 1983, so she had high hopes it would have some information on Isabella. She flicked through the pages, not taking long to find what she was looking for.

…The Bree family had lived happily at Evesham Hall for many years until one Christmas tragedy had struck, their young daughter, Isabella, only 7 years of age, fell through the ice on the lake and drowned. The mother, Beverly, struck down by grief, had taken her own life. Soon after, her husband, Andrew, sold the house and moved to London, little is known about what happened to him after that. Local folklore states that Isabella still roams the corridors of Evesham Hall, looking for her mother…

Rachael sighed, her heart in pain at the death of the little girl. She checked out the book, hoping to learn more about her in the future, and made her way over to a heavily decorated little shop. She purchased enormous amounts of decorations; lights, a tree, tinsel, even a little nativity scene. The white haired gentleman behind the counter offered to look after her purchases until she was finished in town, she would need a taxi to get it all back.

Her final stop was a small toy shop, which the woman at the library had told her about when Rachael had enquired, called *Araminta's Toy Emporium.* She pushed open the door into the warmth, and a young, handsome man with black shaggy hair and beautiful big brown eyes looked up at her. She could have sworn he was a bit startled as he looked up from his book and then clumsily stood up.

"Hello there, er, Happy Christmas! Welcome to Aramintas, as you can probably guess I'm, in fact, not Araminta, she is my mother. My name is Christopher, er, Chris. How can I help?"

Rachael unknowingly blushed, she was not used to male attention, and she definitely fancied this young man. "Hi Chris, i'm looking for a little teddy rabbit if you have one, preferably white?"

Chris leapt into action, searching around the nooks and crannies of the packed toy store. It was beautiful, with a huge red train set the centre piece, a child's paradise.

"Im very sorry, I don't think we have any rabbits, maybe you could try the city, theres a huge toy store in the centre, it's about an hour away, or I could try and order one for you, what's your name?"

Rachael gave Chris her name and address, and the two of them ended up chatting for longer than she intended - it was beginning to get dark but she was no longer worried as she was to get a taxi. Chris was a charming, good looking lad, and what Rachael did not realise was he had been stunned by her beauty the moment he had met her. The more they chatted, the more he liked her, although confused by her shyness. She did not seem like the type of girl who lacked male attention, yet she was timid, she had no one. He couldn't believe it when she said she was to spend Christmas alone.

PART 4

Christmas

Isabella waited at the window, watching as the frosty night began to set in, Rachael had promised she would be back by night time, was she going to leave her behind, just like her Mum.

As headlights appeared through the mist, Isabella's little heart jumped with joy. She watched Rachael drag huge shopping bags through the snow up to the front door, confused as to why the nasty taxi driver was not helping her new friend.

Once Rachael had finished her trips back and forth from the taxi, she paid the taxi driver off, making sure not to tip the grumpy old fart. She shut the front door behind her, closing out the shrieking wind. She spun around and saw Isabella rushing cheerfully down the stairs. She was overcome with emotion for the little girl, a tear in her eye. She knelt down to Isabella's height and put her arms around her.

"I was so worried you were not going to come back, that you were going to leave me in the big house like everyone else." Said Isabella as she hugged her back, not ready to let her go.

"I'm not going anywhere Bel, you are stuck with me now, now come on, lets get some of these decorations up, it's not too late to have a lovely Christmas together."

Isabella leant back and gave her a huge smile, tears in her eyes as well, but this time tears of joy. It was a truly beautiful moment. Rachael watched as her little Christmas miracle ran over to the shopping and started inspecting all the decorations.

They spent the rest of the evening decorating the house

together. Whilst the building was far too big to decorate the whole thing, they focused on the kitchen and the living room as well as Isabella's room. Rachael was not sure if the girl actually slept, but she wanted to make it as special as she could for her.

When they were finished, Rachael watched as Isabella stood on a chair and put the little star on top of their enormous tree, then turned to face her with a little grin that showed her happiness with her accomplishment.

Rachael had bought some wood whilst she was in town, and lit a roaring fire in the old fire place. She took the sheets off one of the sofas, and pushed it close to the fire. Isabella came and joined her, resting her head on Rachaels shoulder. Rachael put her arm around her, the girls frozen skin unusually comforting in front of the blazing heat. Bel drifted off to sleep, and as Rachael looked at her again, she had vanished. Rachael smiled, content in the knowledge that the girl would be back in the morning.

Rachael awoke on a glisteningly sunny Christmas morning to the sound of a car driving away. She looked at the window and was too late to catch the face of the driver. Confused, she wrapped her dressing gown around her and made her way to the front door.

She pushed open the front door and shivered as the soft snow fell in front of her. At her feet was a little box, wrapped up in Christmassy wrapping paper that showed little smiling penguins dressed up in Santa Hats. It had been a long time since she had had a present to open on Christmas day. A card was attached to the present and she gently ripped it open.

Hey Rachael
It was lovely meeting you yesterday.
I thought this little guy could keep you company today.
My mum is away this Christmas, so I have no on to share a
Turkey with this year. My number is 01825 634571, if you
fancy, I could bring one over later today?
Have a lovely day
Chris
(From the toy shop)

Rachael caught herself with an enormous grin on her face, she was beginning to love this place. She picked up the present and tore off the wrapping paper, completely forgetting she was still stood out in the cold.

A box lay beneath it, and she opened it, and what she saw bought a joy to get that she had not felt in a very, very long time.

A little white rabbit looked back at her, its stitched mouth smiling at her, pleased to have found a loving home.

Rachael turned round, and saw Isabella looking down in her familiar position at the top of the stairs, the little girl glaring curiously at the box in Rachaels hand. Rachael laughed and handed the box over to her.

"Happy Christmas Bel," she said as she gave her another warm embrace. She smiled as the girl frantically opened the box. Her little hand pulled the rabbit out of the box, her faced completely overjoyed, Tears again rolling down her tiny cheeks. Bel hugged the rabbit tight, "Is she for me? I love her so much! can I call her Snowbell?" She said frantically as she smiled at Rachael, coming back into her arms as she cuddled her new furry friend.

Rachael nodded and laughed, noticing that a tear was rolling down her face as well, then she made her way over to the telephone....

Dream Girl

"Of all the things you choose in life, you don't get to choose what your nightmares are. You don't pick them; they pick you."

- John Irving

DREAM GIRL

Where did she come from? She was beautiful, more beautiful than anyone I had ever seen before. Her eyes, which looked like emeralds, expensive emeralds, were fixed upon mine. She glided towards me, the swarm of people around her moving out the way.

Where am I? I could not take me eyes of her, she was getting closer now. I could feel heat travel through my body, and my throat tightened as she came closer. The people around us seemingly oblivious to her beauty.

As she neared me, her full, scarlet lips twisted into a smile, with long rusty orange hair falling down the sides of her head. She had freckles too, dotted all over her clear, tanned cheeks. She reached out her hand as she came closer.

I felt my heartbeat quicken, I had never in my life seen a woman as perfect as the one in front of me. As I took her hand In mine, and then the other one, I felt my body coarse with a need for her, like nothing in the world mattered anymore except having her.

She came to stop in front of me, she was shorter than me, but not by much, and her eyes continued to stare into mine. They did not blink, they were focused and intense, but I loved it, I could have stayed there for ever, perhaps I would.

She had no shoes on , her feet covered in sand. A beach, we must be on a beach. Perhaps it was a beach party, that would explain all the people. I dared not look away from her, in case when I looked back she was gone, I did not care where I was, as long as she was here with me. Why am I here alone? Where are my friends? I did not care, for the only person I want to be with is this girl in front of me.

I tried to talk, but words seemed to get stuck in my throat. I wanted to ask her everything, what was her name, where she came from, why she has come over to me like this? Instead, I allowed myself to simply enjoy the moment. It was euphoric, I felt an electricity between us, like we were two magnets that had just been pulled together.

She let go of one of my hands, and I worried that she was going, but she put her soft palm on my cheek. Her skin felt warm, welcoming, I wondered whether I should kiss her, but I was paralysed by her beauty, unable to do anything but watch her, feel her.

The world around us started to disappear, and the only thing that was left was the two of us, her hand on my cheek, our eyes locked in an eternal stare. I felt intoxicated by her, consumed by her. I wanted to hold her close, I wanted to kiss her.

I closed my eyes, pushing my head towards hers. But there was nothing there, and when I opened my eyes, she was gone.

*

As I woke up I felt my heart instantly sink as I realised she was not with me anymore. The dream was fresh in my mind, the image of her beauty emblazoned in my head. I was afraid to focus on anything else, in case the memory never returned. I resigned myself to the fact that I would never see her again.

I sat up, my head still in a tailspin. I looked around at my room, I was alone as usual. I had grown messy lately, yesterdays dinner sat on my bedside table, unfinished. I had not had much of an appetite. I picked my suit up off the bedroom floor, my shirt had a stain on it, but I did not care, I would wear it anyway.

My flat felt cold and empty. The world was grey and lifeless compared to the girl in my dream last night, I longed to return, to hold her hand again, to feel her palm against my cheek.

It was not long into the day that I began to forget what she looked like, as you do with dreams, they seep away. I could not focus at work, I felt delirious, haunted by a beautiful memory I was struggling to recall. Everything around me felt dead. I did not care about my job, or about my colleagues. Occasionally throughout the day, people tried to engage me in conversation, but I was not interested.

I was in a trance, staring at my computer, when I heard a voice. It was Craig, who worked in the cubicle next to me. He wanted to know if I fancied a drink after work. That was our routine, we always went for a drink after work.

I decided to go, I needed to get my mind off the girl. The girl that I would never see again. The alcohol destroyed the last bits of memory I had of her. All that was left was the red hair, and the emerald eyes. I could not remember her form, or the shape of her face. It was probably for the best.

Craig had asked if I was alright, that I had seemed pretty low lately. In truth, I have never felt more alone, I desired female company, someone to warm my bed on these cold winter nights. Perhaps, I thought, last night had been a sign from my brain, telling me to get out there, to meet someone. No one would ever be as perfect as the girl from my dream.

I returned home, I only stayed for a couple of drinks. As I went into my flat I once again felt isolated, I wished for some colour to puncture my life. I forced down a microwave carbonara, it was tasteless.

I got into bed, decided against having a wash. I just wanted to sleep, to escape the grey world I was living in, if only for a little bit. I wondered if I would dream again tonight.

*

The music rang in my ears, it was cheerful, upbeat. The acoustic guitar reverberated around the restaurant, as men and women danced around the tables. The women in particular oozed colour, their dresses, their make up, the effect of the sun on their skin. Everyone was happy, having a good time.

I looked around the table I was sitting at, in front of me lay an orange plate with the remains of a steak on it, and across from me was another plate. It looked to have had pasta in it, and beside it was a large wine glass, half full of a crimson liquid. My heart beat faster, I was not alone.

She came out of the toilet, I saw her instantly. How could I not, my eyes were drawn to her. Tonight, her fire coloured hair was tied up on her head, and it complimented her face perfectly. Her cheekbones turned to dimples as she smiled at me.

My heart raced as she walked back to the table. She was wearing a lime green summer dress, and it suited her wonderfully, like she had been dressed by a stylist. She walked slower tonight, more refined, perhaps that was because of the heels she was wearing. I could not help but stare at her, my eyes following every step she made. She looked absolutely stunning, were we on a date?

As she approached the table, she walked behind me, dropping her arms down my shoulders, and gently kissing me on the cheek. This was when I heard her speak for the first time.

"I'm having the most wonderful evening, would you like to dance with me?"

I turned my head to face hers, our eyes locking once again. I tried to talk back, but once again my throat felt locked. She took my hand in hers, her face playful now. She pulled me up, and I allowed my body to be taken by her, pulled into the crowd of happy couples dancing the night away. The music had slowed down now, it was intense, romantic. She held me close, her heels putting her at about the same height as me. I could feel her breath on my cheek, and I could smell her aromatic perfume, it was suffocating.

As we danced, I knew that I never wanted to let go, I never wanted this moment to end. I wanted to be with her forever in this bar, dancing, holding each other.

She leant her head back slightly, and smiled at me. I still could get no words out, but it did not matter, she did not seem to mind. She pushed her lips close to mine, and then they were touching. I felt time stand still, my knees weaken. My whole body felt warm and all my senses exploded. My stomach fluttered as we continued to kiss, and everything else around us slipped away.

I closed my eyes, enjoying the greatest moment of my life. But then when I opened them, the restaurant had vanished, the colours had faded to grey. She was no longer in my arms.

*

The rain crashed into my misty window, the sky outside was overcast and dark. I swore to myself as I realised I had been taken away from her again. I could not believe I had been lucky enough to see her once again, but that made it all the more difficult to lose her for a second time. My greatest dream had become my darkest nightmare.

I needed to be with her, to smell her asphyxiating scent, to have her hand on my cheek, her lips touching mine.

I could not get out of bed, I had no desire to do anything except see her again. I tried to get back to sleep, hoping that the darkness would bring her back to me, but it was not working, I could not sleep. It felt good that I could still remember what she looked like but I wanted her to be in front of me, in bed next to me. I wondered if I would ever see her again.

Part of me knew that it would be for the best if she did not return to my sleep again. It was too difficult to accept that she was not there when I woke up.

The rain continued to hammer onto the window, piercing the eerie silence that surrounded me as I lay in bed. It was the afternoon now, I had not gone to work. My phone vibrated every now and again, it must be my manager or Craig. I did not care, I could not go to work today, I could not risk losing the memory of this woman. Dreams slipped away quickly, and I was not sure if she would return to me again. I did not even know her name, this gorgeous woman who had become a part of me.

I felt my stomach rumble, it needed food, so I crept out of bed into the kitchen. The dusty fridge was empty. I headed down to the shop, and bought myself a chicken mayonnaise sandwich. It tasted stale, lifeless. I realised that I was not hungry for food, but hungry for something else, for love, for affection, for her.

It was getting dark and cold now, I had done nothing today except think about her. I finally looked at my phone, Craig said he had covered for me at work, but I would need to be back on Monday. It must be Friday today, and the weekend scared me, stuck in my empty flat, just with the image of her. This time I had not forgotten her, she was stamped in my mind. It stopped me concentrating on anything else, I could not even turn the TV on.

Eventually I got back into bed, the rain had stopped and the silence had well and truly set in. Sleep excited me, as I could possibly see her again. When I was asleep, I was no longer alone.

*

I felt her palm locked in mine, we were walking. The temperature was warm, and there was a beautiful blood orange sun set over the top of the low building lining the side of the pavement. I looked down at her, and was once again stunned by her. She looked back at me, squeezing my hand a little as she gazed back at me. Her freckles today were more prominent, she had no make up on - but she still looked glorious. She wore a baggy red t shirt over the top of some denim shorts. Every time I saw her she looked incredible. I wondered where we were going, as the last dregs of sunlight disappeared from the streets.

We arrived at what must be her apartment, as she let go of my hand and rustled around in her pink handbag, eventually pulling out a set of keys, which she turned in the lock, pushing open the door and then taking my hand again and pulling me inside.

I felt myself tense up as she led me upstairs to her bedroom. It was spotless the sandy coloured walls littered with various paintings and photos of her. The bed, sat in the middle of the room, with multicoloured sheets laid out perfectly over the mattress. She lit a candle on the bedside table, dimming the lights. She put on some music, it was similar to the music in the restaurant. Slow, romantic, intense.

She came over to me, and once again I felt myself suffocating, she took off my shirt, and ran her hands down my chest. Her skin was so smooth, and it felt good. My body was weakening, but my brain was screaming with excitement. I had never wanted someone so much. Words still eluded me.

Her hands rose from my chest to my face, and she kissed me again, this time more passionately. I felt breathless as her tongue entered my mouth, I put my arms around her body and pulled her in, but she escaped, and headed backwards to the bed, pulling me down with her.

I scrambled on top of her, my hands were now guiding themselves. I pulled her t shirt over her head, and then reached round her back and unclipped her bra. My hands found their way onto her breasts, and as I touched her nipples her kisses become harder, more intense.

My heart is racing now, I desire her so much. She slips off her shorts and her pants, and her naked body lies on the bed, ready for me. It is bewitching. Mesmerising. She wants me as well.

I take off my trousers, and now I am naked as well. I climb on

*top of her, and then I am inside her. She groans with pleasure, as her
fingernails drive into my back, scratching up and down as I make love
to her.*

*It is not long before she has reached a climax and then I join her.
The whole moment is electric, like nothing I have ever felt before. I
close my eyes as I finish inside her, her body is warm and sweaty. I feel
completely euphoric. I am so in love with her.*

When I open my eyes, she is gone.

*

I opened my eyes, and I saw my white, cracked ceiling, and
immediately my heart sank. I looked to my right, and the bed was
empty, the charcoal sheets crumpled and bare. A rage took over
my body, and I felt like screaming, but much like in my dreams,
nothing came out.

I felt a surge of anger towards my brain, why was it doing this
to me? Taking me to this place every night only to tear it away
from me the next morning. I no longer wished to return to the cold
reality of my life.

I knew there would be no chance of getting back to sleep, of
returning to her apartment, returning to her arms.

It was Saturday today, and I was alone. I looked out through
the morning mist on my window. The rain had stopped, but it was
a gloomy, overcast day. The first thing I saw was a young couple,
wrapped up warm in big wooly jumpers, laughing as they walked
down the pavement. They're happiness angered me. It was not
long ago that I had their joy at being together, even if it was in my
dreams, and now it had been taken from me.

Every day that I woke up without her was getting harder and
harder. Initially, her image would deteriorate as the day went on -
but now it was lodged at the forefront of my mind, until I went to
sleep and then I would be reunited with her.

I went to the shop, but this time not for a sandwich. I bought
a crate of beers, and a bottle of whiskey, and then returned to the
solitude of my flat.

It was only ten in the morning, but I could not stand it
anymore. Last night with her had been too much, too memorable,

I could not be without her. I would drink myself to sleep today.

I switched off my phone - my sister Eve had been trying to call me, it was my nephew's birthday today, I was supposed to be at the party. I had not even bought a present, I did not care.

I drank all day, but it did not make it an easier. The more drunk I got, the more she festered in my mind. I felt anxiety about work, about missing the birthday party, and the alcohol made it worse. Made it more difficult.

I thought about stopping, what could would It do for me? I was throwing my life away over a girl that I only saw when I was asleep. I found that I could not stop, I was determined to get back to sleep, to be back with her. I would do whatever it took to be back with her.

As night drew in, the flat became shrouded in darkness. I stumbled over to my bed, falling into it with a bang. It was not long before I passed out.

*

The words came out of my mouth before I could catch them, but they felt right, and they felt exciting.

"Lets get married?"

We were back on the beach, and it was dusk, a majestic sunset. Plumes of orange ran across the sky, twisting through the rising darkness of the moon.

Her head was on my chest, and my hand was running through her soft hair. The question caused her to leap up, her body rolling around so her elbows were on my chest. She smiled at me, the dimples that melted my heart every time.

She pushed her head forward and kissed me, before she started giggling, and a tear rolled down her cheek.

"Of course I will, but let's do it now." She said, then pulled me up. My mind raced, my body flush with excitement. We were going to get married.

We headed back to her apartment, and she tried on a few different dresses. She did not have any white dresses but that did not matter, she looked breathtaking in every single one. She eventually decided on the lime green dress that she had worn at the restaurant where we had our first kiss. Every time I looked at her I felt my body weaken, my heart beat faster.

On the way to the registry office, I stopped to buy a bouquet of red roses from a street salesman, and she kissed me as I gave them to her. Everything seemed in fast forward, a blur of excitement and passion. We laughed and held hands the whole way to the registry office.

The ceremony was short, but perfect. We held hands and stared into each others eyes as we said the words, "I do," and the kiss transported me to another world. She had wrapped her hands around my neck, and she was almost laughing as she kissed me. It was the most passionate experience I had ever felt.

She held onto the flowers as we skipped out of the registry office, and threw them out into the empty streets. We did not need anyone else to catch the bouquet, we had each other, and that was all we would ever need.

We found a jewellery shop, but it was closed. I rapped my fist on the window, love drunk and feeling like I could do anything. An elderly lady opened the door, and she laughed as I showed her our wedding certificate. No words were needed.

I picked out a wedding ring covered in emeralds that matched her eyes, and slid it onto her wedding finger. It was a perfect fit. Tears streamed down her cheeks as she looked at it, and it was not long before they fell out of my eyes also.

She led me back to her apartment, still hand in hand, and when we got to the front door she stopped, wrapping her arms around me once again.

"I love you so much, thank you for the best day" she said, before pressing her soft lips against mine.

Then she disappeared into the apartment. When I went in after her, my heart stopped as there was nothing behind the door.

*

My heart ached as my eyes opened. In my other life I was a married man, who had enjoyed the most passionate of weddings. In the real world, I was hungover and alone. I felt completely hopeless, and that in my real life I would never be able to achieve that kind of happiness.

I decided not to turn my phone on, what good would that do. It was a murky morning once again , and my head was swimming with beautiful memories that haunted my every second. I wanted to be with her forever, this life was not working for me.

I felt completely disconnected from the world around me, and I had no intention of going back to it. I had made up my mind, and it had not been a difficult decision. I wanted to be with her forever, she was everything. I wanted my dreams to become a reality and the only way to do that would be to be asleep forever.

My life was not worth living, not when the other option was a life with her.

I headed out to the pharmacy, and picked up as many painkillers as they would allow me to buy, and then after that I bought some more booze. I wanted it to be as painless as possible. A simple transition into the other life. The better life.

On my journey I saw the same young couple from yesterday, they laughed and joked as they walked towards me down the streets. This time I did not feel any anger towards them, I simply was excited to be like them, to join them in blissful happiness.

Back at the flat, I decided to write a brief note. I addressed it to my sister, she was all I really had left.

I'M SORRY EVE. GONE TO A BETTER PLACE. TO BE WITH THE WOMAN OF MY DREAMS. I LOVE YOU.

I knew that she would not understand, why would she? She had no idea what I had been going through. She had no idea how perfect my life was going to be with the girl from my dreams. She would be jealous if she knew.

I sat down on the bed, and started swigging the bottle of whisky that I had. It relaxed me, made me ready for what I had to do. In all honesty I was not scared, why would I be scared of going to see the woman that I loved. The woman that made me happy?

I looked around at my flat, the bland, uninspiring interior was soon to be traded for a beautiful life full of colour and happiness.

I placed all the painkillers into a half pint glass, it was basically full. That would be enough to make my voyage a permanent one. I could not wait to be with her, to see the next instalment of our life together.

I smiled, warmth filling my body. I took the cup of pills, and felt them roll down my throat, and then washed them down with the whisky. I lay back on the bed, it was not long before the darkness took hold of me.

*

A man pushed past me, swearing as I got in his way. The streets were dark, and it was raining. In my hand I had a bag full of shopping, it looked like food. I looked around, she was not with me. Where was she?

I did not know where I was, or where I lived, and the weather was getting worse, the rain soaking through my jacket onto my shirt. It did not quell my excitement, my excitement to see her.

Although I was seemingly lost, my legs appeared to be leading me to a destination. It must be where we lived. We were no longer on the beach, in the sun. But that did not matter, all that mattered was her.

I arrived outside a charcoal door, and I pushed my hands into my pockets, gratefully feeling the cold steel of the keys. I pulled them out, and thrust them into the lock, they slid in seamlessly, and I clicked open the lock. I pushed the door open and ambled in. The house was still, and quiet.

The decorations were minimal. The walls were white, with only a couple of paintings lining them. The furniture was mainly black or navy blue, and uninspiring. There were no photos of us anywhere. Perhaps we had just moved in, and we had much work to do. There was no way she would allow our home to be this bland.

Panicking slightly, I checked my ring finger, and breathed a sigh of relief as I saw the ring was still there. It was worn now however, the gold did not glisten like it had the night we got married.

I made my way up the stairs, holding onto the bannister as I rose up them. I wanted to call for her, but I was tongue tied.

In front of me stood another door, and this one was shut, I pushed it open, only to find a bathroom. It was messy, make-up all over the side and water pooling on the floor. The make-up gave me hope, it was not mine.

I turned back on myself, and headed for the other door upstairs. The door was white, and the handle a dark brown. I wrapped my palm around it, and pushed it open.

I heard the groans instantly, I had heard them before, the night we made love. But it was not me that was causing them.

She was on top of him, riding him. Her hair was no longer the magnificent red, but dyed jet black. She turned to face me, but she was not smiling and she did not stop. She was pale now, and her cheeks gaunt. Her warm eyes had been replaced by a cold stare.

I felt my world turn upside down, and my heart sank. I dropped the keys I was still holding, and turned on my heels, running away. She did not try to stop me.

At the top of the stairs, I tripped and stumbled, falling down them. Then the world went black.

*

The sunlight stung my eyes as they opened. As the world around me started to open up, I started to make out the silhouettes of people stood over me. Soon after, the colour washed into their features.

My sister stood at the foot of the bed, tears streaking her face, dripping down onto her red shirt. Her strawberry blonde hair was tied up on her head. I watched as she breathed a sigh of relief as I opened my eyes.

I was in a hospital, and suddenly the memories of what I had done flooded back into my mind. I remembered standing at the foot of the bed, watching her with someone else. I felt the anger boil inside me, I never wanted to see her again. I thought that I would be with her eternally, but now that would be the worst punishment.

I knew that I would need to find happiness in this world, rather than chase a woman I knew did not exist. I felt stupid, embarrassed, and I knew that no one would understand why I had chosen to do what I had done. But that did not matter anymore.

My sister came over and held my hand, her palms were warm against my cold skin. I welcomed her affection, I would need her now more than ever. Why had I not turned to her when I needed her. I realised that all I needed when I felt so isolated was to reach out to the people that love me, that care about me.

She offered to have me stay at her house for the time being, which I accepted with a smile. Her love injected some warmth into me that I had not felt outside of my dreams.

The woman from my dreams still haunted me, however her bewitching beauty was forgotten, replaced by the image of her with the other man. The blandness of our home, the darkness of the dream, stuck in my mind for a long time.

It was not long before I fell back to sleep. I was tired, and my body was drained after the damage I had done to it.

When I slept, however, I did not dream of her. She had haunted me long enough, and now my mind was rejecting her. When I woke again the sun was shining again through the window, and I felt relief. This reality was not so horrible anymore.

I hoped one day to find love, to find passion like I shared with the woman I met in my sleep. But she was not my dream girl.

She was a drug, and I would have done anything to get a fix. It nearly destroyed my life. I would not allow that to happen again.

Whisky and the Dark Woods

"The walls of isolation are not as solid as your suffering makes them seem"

- Deepak Chopra

PART 1

Chris

He would be back, he always came back, right? Maybe this time I had gone too far, said too much. How could I be a father when I can't even get the kid to stay in the same damn room as me for more than ten minutes.

I looked out the rattling windows at the dark, unforgiving site of the woods that encircled my cabin. They cut me off from society, which I liked. I hated people, hated this new world. The only technology I had time for was my trusty wireless. The only time I left my self imposed exile was to get food and new batteries when my sidekick ran out of juice.

I did love my son Chris. He hated me. He blamed the break up of his childhood home on me and I could understand why. About 6 years ago, when Chris was 11, I had ended one of my many benders in the arms of another woman. Empty bottles on the floor, powder on the bedside table, life in the gutter.

I could never understand why my ex wife, Tess, even bought the boy round anymore. She wasn't exactly a mother crafted by the Gods, and I am pretty sure she bought him here when she couldn't find a sitter for her forays into town with her girlfriends. For Christ sake, Chris was 17 now, couldn't he look after himself?

I poured myself a whiskey, cursing as I realised the ice bucket was empty, and slouched into my creaky rocking chair. A rocking chair, aged 40? No wonder he hated coming here. His Dad was a liquor soaked loser who spent his life sat in a chair designed for a retired old man listening to the fucking radio.

No TV, no phone reception, no game station or what ever the hell it was called, and the only company he had was a man who had basically ruined his life. A man who clearly had no intention of getting himself out of this rut.

I looked back on our latest argument. Chris had, to his credit, made an effort to actually try and get me to do something. His mother had been teaching him how to cook, and he wanted me to drive him to the shops so we could buy some food and he could cook dinner. Earlier, he had looked in the fridge and grunted as he surveyed the only options - 2 microwave carbonara's and a frozen pizza. A frozen pizza with mushrooms on it. Chris fucking hated mushrooms.

His mother was a great chef, and the food at our broken family home was something that I missed dearly. The idea of a cooked meal that had stemmed from Tess' training should have been a no brainer, but the Whiskey had other ideas. I couldn't afford to lose my license. Nobody delivered out here, not even a milkman. I needed my old pick up to make my weekly trip to the shop. I was way over the limit.

The road through the woods also went straight past the entrance to Reardon maximum security prison, meaning there was always police out on the roads. Reardon was home to some of our countries most notorious rapists and murderers.

Somehow, it had felt right that I resided close to the scum of the earth. I could never decide if that was because it made me feel better about myself or because I fitted in with other people that had needlessly thrown their life away.

"Sorry kid, you should have asked earlier, I've had a few of these now and you know what the Old Bill's like round here, can't you just be happy with that carbonara, bought that 'specially for you didn't I."

As If that was a fucking treat, what was I thinking. Chris burst into his usual rampage, accusing me of ruining his life, telling me what a waste of space I was. Usually I tried to soften the situation, but tonight I was in no mood, the whiskey had taken hold of me.

"If nothing I do makes you happy, you ungrateful little shit, then why don't you fuck off out of my house."

Tears formed under Chris's bright blue eyes, and he ran out

the door. Chris had built a number of Dens in the woods over the years. I thought of them as retreats, places where he could escape from his completely unreasonable father. He always went to them after our fights, in the summer he even slept in them, only coming to the house to get some water or a new book from my miserable looking bookshelf.

I knew the reason why these words came out of my mouth was the booze, but the fact of the matter was I always regretted it, I just couldn't stop myself. I was so overcome with hate and misery, and Chris was the only person around when it came out of my mouth. I loved the boy, but I couldn't stop myself from being as horrible as possible to him at every bloody waking moment.

I thought about going out to talk to him, like I always did, then sighed and decided against it, and poured another drink. Like I always did. The whiskey soothed my temper as I rocked back on my chair.

I had not taken any drugs in a long time. Not for want of trying, I just couldn't get hold of it out here in the woods. My old dealer, Paul, was long gone. I could really do with a line. I missed the euphoria that alcohol couldn't give me. The escape. I always thought about cocaine after our fights. This time was no different.

The thought passed, I poured another Whiskey, more or less a quadruple measure. I was beginning to feel a bit pissed now. I fumbled around in my pockets for my Chesterfields and lit one, took a big drag into my lungs.

The sad thing was, this was my happy place. My son crying in the woods because of me, and me sat on my fucking rocking chair, drunk as a skunk, listening to Billy Big Bollocks talk about their college football team's chances at breaking some pointless record.

PART 2

The Woods

We interrupt this bulletin to bring you a breaking news story. An inmate of Reardon prison, a Mr Craig Poulter, has escaped from the facility. Mr Poulter is considered armed and very dangerous. We advise all residents of the Reardon area to lock their doors and windows and not answer the door to anyone. Mr Poulter is 5'11, Caucasian, skinhead with a tattoo of a teardrop under his left eye. The police are doing everything they can to keep the situation under control but we must ask the public to be vigilante, and above all, be safe.

I jerked up, knocking my Whiskey glass onto the floor. I swore under my breathe, but I knew for once I had to go and do what any good father would do, make sure their son is inside when there is a fucking murderer on the loose in the woods!

I was out in the woods quite a bit hunting rabbits, usually when I was too drunk to go to the shop, so I knew where Chris' dens were. I staggered out of the house, looking over at the path that led into the woods. The huge trees looked back at me, disapprovingly.

One by one I checked his dens. Small wooden structures crafted out of fallen forestry, all of them together looked like someone had made a little village for a community of dwarves.

My heart was beginning to beat faster, all the dens so far had been empty. There was one left, but I couldn't hear any noise coming out of it, not that reading was a a particularly loud activity.

This one was obviously his latest one, it rose higher than the others, and the craftsmanship on it was surprisingly good, rather than being the shape of a teepee like the others, this one was an actual box. I shouted his name, no response. There was a pile of logs out the front where it looked like Chris had planned on lighting a fire.

Cautiously, I creeped round to the front of it and pushed aside the bedsheet that made a makeshift door.

Fuck. Nothing

I shouted his name again. Nothing.

Night time was coming in, surely Chris wasn't out deeper in the woods at this time. It was a windy, cold night. Darkness enshrouded his den. Darkness that I only thought enshrouded me.

I looked back into the den one last time and my heart sunk. His phone was on top of the book he had been reading. Even though there was no signal out here, I knew Chris wouldn't go anywhere without his phone. Nobody does these days.

I sobered up quickly, alcohol, for the first time in a while, at the back of my mind. I ran back into the house and grabbed my hunting rifle and some ammo. I couldn't find my knife so I settled on taking the empty bottle of whiskey, it would cause some damage if I had to drive it into someones head. Finally, I found my torch, cursing as it didn't turn on. I sacrificed the batteries from my radio and the beam from the torch illuminated the front room.

I had Chris's phone just in case it got any signal and I could call the police. I had already nailed the password - his Mum's birthday.

I hurried into the darkness, The torch just about showing the path into the woods. I went back past the dens, checking again to make sure Chris hadn't returned. Nothing.

I knew Chris had an axe out here which I had begrudgingly given him a few years ago to chop wood for his fires. It occurred to me that he didn't have it with him. It warmed me to know that he had some form of protection.

I went deeper into the woods. Every time I heard a bird cry or the rustle from the animal my heart leaped. It was cold but I was sweating, all the booze escaping my body like the murderer escaping Reardon prison. I was no tracker, it had been dry so there was no chance of footprints.

An hour went by, and still no sign of my son. The son I had

let down over and over again. I felt tears in my eyes, I could not handle again being the cause of something happening to him.

I heard the soft stream of the small river that ran through the woods. I was thirsty now, my mouth dry from all the cigarettes and whiskey. I cupped my hands together and drank, the dirty water surprisingly refreshing. I splashed some on my face to try and clear my head a bit. I had to think, had to listen.

My mind went back to the argument, sending the boy out, sending him into the arms of a murderer.

PART 3

Blood

I was deep into the woods now, I do not think I had ever been this far in before. Scared and anxious, I looked at my watch. 11pm. I had been out here for almost 4 hours now. The ground was frosty, and the trees continued to stare at me, judging me for all the terrible decisions I had made.

There was no path anymore, I may as well accept the fact that I was now lost. I couldn't let myself be scared, I needed to be strong for my son.

BANG

I swivelled around, my pulse quickened. That was a gunshot.

It was back the way I had came. It was clear, but it definitely was not that close. I made my way back, finding the river again and following it as a guide.

Animals were rushing around me, clearly spooked by the gunshot that I had heard. It had only been one, implying that whoever had shot had clearly hit their target. Please let it not be Chris.

I kept my torch shined on the ground in front of me. The animals concealed my sound, but the torch would surely give away my position. I quickly checked Chris's phone, no signal.

Two deer flew past me, and then a rabbit. They must be running away from something, I thought, so I summoned all the courage I had and made my way in the opposite direction from them. I was still travelling parallel to the river as if it was a fucking bannister.

Thirsty again, I stopped crouched down at the water. I shone my torch on the water trying to see if there was any that was remotely clean, but what I saw made me recoil back in horror.

The water that floated past me was a crimson red. Lots of crimson red. I had showered enough after slaughtering rabbits and various bar fights to know exactly what that crimson red was. It was blood. There was so much of it that it had to be human blood.

Terrified now, I traced the stream a bit further upriver. The blood flow constant and menacing in the water.

My torch uncovered an unnatural looking shape propped up on the river bank on the other side. I lowered myself into the cold water and crossed over, the torch light slowly illuminating the horrific scene in front of me.

The lifeless man lay face up. It wasn't Chris.

I surveyed the scene, my heart pounding. The man was wearing a security uniform, and his service revolver had gone, and if he had a radio, that was gone too. He had been shot just once in the heart, the work of someone who had killed before.

His face looked back at me. A man who had made something of his life, who had a job and looked after the community, ruthlessly killed. He did not deserve this, Chris did not deserve this, if anyone deserved to die today it was me.

If the danger of the situation had not yet fully dawned on me, now it hit me like a train, could I really do this?

Craig Poulter had obviously snuck up on this man, overpowered him, taken his weapon and then shot him. The same fate could await my son. What good would an axe do against a loaded fucking weapon? My head was spinning. The only thing I had in this world was my son, and even though he hated me, I had to save him.

I closed the policeman's eyes and dragged him out of the river, it seemed the right thing to do, then pressed on. Poulter had to be close, the gun shot was only 15 minutes ago.

PART 4

Craig Poulter

I recalled hearing about this man when he got taken into prison. It had been all over the radio. His wife had been sleeping with another man and Poulter had gone round to the victims house and put a shotgun shell in the chest of the man, and then one in his wife and the man's son for good measure. The son had been 15, clearly Poulter had no problem killing kids.

I was beginning to give up hope when I heard a loud noise that blocked out everything else, it was getting closer. A helicopter.

I ran and found a clearing in the trees. The helicopter was landing, I could now make out that it was a police chopper.

I ran closer to the scene, making sure I kept out of site, had they found Craig?

The adrenaline was pumping now as I got closer to the scene. I tripped over a root, the hard frost floor painful on my weak knees. The bullets in my pocket spilt out all over the place. As I picked them up, I swore as I realised that in my drunken stupor earlier I had picked up the box of blanks rather than the live ammo. What good would they be.

I got back up on my feet and wiped myself down. What the hell was I doing. How was I going to take on an armed murderer with an empty hunting rifle and an empty bottle of sodding whisky. I could only hope the police got to him first. I did not know for sure that he had my son but I feared the worst.

I edged closer to the helicopter and I began to hear muffled shouts. Something was happening.

Finally I got to were the woods had opened up enough for the helicopter to land. I looked up over a bush and I saw the sight that will no doubt haunt my dreams for years to come.

Chris had a gun to his temple, and behind him stood the terrifying figure of Craig Poulter. It had to be him, I was not close enough to make out the tear drop tattoo, but who else could it have been.

"Don't come any closer or the kid fucking gets it" shouted Poulter.

In front of him stood four armed policeman, looking very nervous. Poulter was pulling Chris back towards the woods, obviously he was using the boy as foil for another escape. Had Chris been there when Poulter had killed the security guard? Surely the sight would mess the boy up even more. I felt sick.

Thinking quickly, and probably suicidally, I slowly made my way round the tree line, so I was close to where Poulter would back into the trees.

Chris was crying, the fear etched in his face. I had to do something. I grasped the Whiskey bottle in my hand, and crept up behind Poulter.

One of the officers, a young lad who could not be more than 25, caught sight of me. He remained still, obviously anticipating what I had to do.

Poulter edged back towards me, still with no idea I was there. I knew this was my moment. With the adrenaline racing through my body, i grabbed the mans right arm from behind and shoved it up. A shot rang out into the sky as my left arm smashed the whiskey bottle into the mans head.

The connection was pure and sweet. Blood spattered over me. Poulter dropped like a brick.

Chris, who had jumped on the floor, looked at me, completely startled. The shock in his eyes said it all. I fell to my knees, the tears f lowing now, whilst the police raced forward and cuffed Poulter.

I held my son to my chest, and he hugged me back. It felt incredible. We both cried, no words said, no words needed. I would never let him down again, never tell him to go away. I would be a father to him now.

I looked down at the smashed whiskey bottle on the floor. The whiskey bottle that had ruined my life. The whiskey bottle that had saved my sons life. The irony.

Missing In Paradise

"I am not the same, having seen the moon shine on the other side of the world"

- Mary Anne Radmacher

PROLOGUE

The cool turquoise sea brushed gently against Sally's sandy feet, the soft whooshing of the water taking her momentarily away from the extreme hunger and thirst that she had been struggling to keep at bay.

She ran her hand through her rough, dreadlocked hair. Her fingers felt thin, her skin callous. She picked up her coconut shell - it had rained the night before, a rare luxury, and so she had used the coconut shells to collect some rainwater. The fluids on her lips made her feel euphoric, if only for a fraction of a second.

The blazing sun tortured her skin, but she had grown used to the punishment, and now welcomed it - she enjoyed the cooling feeling that her body felt when she re entered the shade, and she liked the sensation of the salty water massaging her toes.

She thought about her husband, and then the guilt came.

CHAPTER 1

A Fall From Grace

When Sally's best friend Miranda had suggested a holiday to the Seychelles, Sally had thought it was a wonderful idea. She had grown tired of the hustle and bustle of London, and her perfect relationship with her husband, George, had become strained.

Sally was a writer, but her mind had become clouded, unable to generate ideas - it was beginning to trouble her, leading her down a stressful path that seemed a long way away when she had been in Waterstones signing copies of her bestseller only eighteen months ago.

Her novel, entitled *Whiskey and the Dark Woods*, had taken her to a level beyond her wildest dreams. She had tapped into a period of her life where drink and drugs had ruled her, a place that seemed perilously close again.

She had been drinking again, every day now, the drinks getting larger as the inspiration diminished.

The royalties she gained from her release allowed her to buy an apartment in Onslow Square, between Chelsea and South Kensington. She loved it at first, but now her dream home seemed to sap her of her energy. The whirring of vehicles and buses, and the noisy stampede of humans around her only distracting her from her follow up hit.

Her relationship with George had also suffered in their new surroundings. They had married at a small ceremony five years previously, at the beautiful Cripps Barn in the Cotswolds, and he had been incredibly supportive of her talents, always believed in her.

He worked as an account manager for a publishing company in London, and it was George who had pushed his company, *Artistic License,* to take on Sally's script, eventually getting it on shelves around the world.

As the money came in, their old place in East Grinstead, near Brighton, had become an annoyance with the daily commute they both now had to make.

The first few months had been amazing, romantic dinners at some of Londons hottest restaurants, cuddling up in the mornings now that they had the extra time, and exploring their new city on the weekends.

But lately, the stress Sally felt had caused her to isolate, punishing herself for her lack of ideas. She did not go out, did not make love to her husband, merely locked herself away in her office, cradling a glass of wine and staring at a blank computer screen.

George was now regularly out late with his friends, terrified to come home to his irritable wife. When he did come home, she would always find a reason to tell him off - which led to him often sleeping on the sofa, which he did not enjoy. George loved his wife but felt like he did not know this woman that he now lived with.

He longed for the woman he married, Sally Cranston, with her beautiful flowing blonde hair, her piercing sapphire blue eyes, her perfect smile and her incredible sense of adventure.

Little did he know, Sally longed for that person as well, she hated herself for how she treated her husband, but the pressure she put on herself, coupled with the alcohol, had turned her into a woman that she despised.

Her best friend Miranda, in particular, had grown concerned for Sally's wellbeing, and after a number of failed attempts, had finally managed to extract her from her isolation. It saddened her that she had to use the promise of alcohol, but it appeared to be the only way to get Sally to leave her apartment and open up.

Sally had arrived at *Moonlight,* a bar on Walton Street, near her home, looking pale and tired. Miranda bought them a bottle of champagne which was followed by some strong gin and tonic chasers.

Eventually, Sally had broken down, releasing her feelings to her friend - her anxiety, her loneliness, and her stress all caused by her inability to write anything, and the pressure from her publisher to follow up her novel. Sally wept as she spoke about her self induced alienation from her husband, and her return to the murky depths of alcoholism.

She was a shadow of Miranda's beautiful, fun loving best friend.

Miranda thought long and hard about Sally's problems, and decided that the best thing for her would be to get away, to a place quiet and far away from here, and unwind. The idea seemed to brighten Sally, a small flame flickered in her eye for the first time in a long time.

As they scrolled through destinations on Sally's cracked iPhone screen, one place stuck out - the Seychelles.

CHAPTER 2

Paradise

George thought it was a great idea, and he hoped that when she returned he would have his wife back. It would give him a bit of space as well, which he felt that he needed.

For the two weeks leading up to Sally's departure, romance returned to their relationship, a part of her old self had returned, the excitement of her upcoming adventure igniting her sullen soul. They shared the same bed, and even made love a few times.

She was happy and hopeful, the horizon suddenly clearing, the fog in her mind dispersing slowly just at the thought of an escape from the misery she had created for herself.

When the day finally came around, George had helped her pack, and taken her to *Heathrow*. They embraced and kissed as he waved goodbye, reminding her that he loved her, and wishing her luck.

She was excited, and this made him feel happy and comfortable. She was going to go there for 4 months, and had found a perfect little apartment overlooking a beach just outside *Victoria,* the small capital city of the island. It seemed like a long time, it was, but she knew the benefits she could potentially get from it.

Sally polished off her gin and looked out the window as the plane descended into the Victoria airport, the island was incredibly beautiful. The glistening blue sea surrounding the lush green hills, the passengers around her marvelling equally at their destination.

The city itself was small, even smaller when compared to London, it looked perfect. The buildings were small and spaced out, and the vehicles on the sandy roads surrounding them were sparse.

She hated flying, but forgot her fears as she gawped at her new home.

The airport was quiet, and she made a quick stop at the bar - excited to try one of the local cocktails. She intended to cut down on her drinking whilst she was out here, but her gin on the plane had wetted her appetite, besides, it was her first day, and she wanted to enjoy it as much as possible.

She drained her *Victoria Fizz,* which the cheerful barman had told her was a concoction of orange juice, sugar, Drambuie and soda water, and located a taxi. The driver spoke a bit of English, and she showed him her destination on her phone. He smiled and set off, humming along to the music blasting out of his radio.

It was September, so it had been cold in the UK when she had left, but the heat she felt on the island was overwhelming. She liked it, and imagined the alcohol sweating out of her, cleansing her of her sins.

Sally smiled as she arrived at her apartment, it was everything she had imagined and more. It looked more of a bungalow, small and picturesque, and surrounded by sand. It was secluded, with a few small dwellings a little further down the dusty road that ran behind the long beach.

She pushed open the wooden front door, which had recently been fitted with a new lock - and took in her new surroundings. The front door led into a small kitchen, painted lime green, with all the basics, a sink, an oven, a small microwave and a hob. It all looked sparklingly clean, and ready to use. An archway from the kitchen led to the sitting area, which had a comfortable looking blue sofa, a small TV, and a desk - she would use that if by some luck a few ideas come to her, she had packed her laptop just in case. The wallpaper was a similar lime green to the kitchen, and on the desk there was a small welcome pack with maps and a couple of menus from local restaurants.

A pair of glass double doors to the left of the TV led out to a wooden porch overlooking the beach, and there was another doorway that led to the small bedroom, hosting a single bed and a surprisingly fresh en suite bathroom hidden behind another pair of sliding doors. She smiled as she saw there was a bath as well as a shower.

Sally, having sussed out where the local store is, spent her first night sitting out on her porch, slowly working her way through a bottle of gin. She felt totally at peace, enjoying a beautiful crimson sunset and the melancholy noise of the waves gently breaking onto the shore.

She kept her troubles at home out of her mind with the Gin, and just soaked up the beautiful atmosphere, looking forward to what her first full day in the Seychelles had in store for her.

CHAPTER 3

Vic's

The first few days Sally spent exploring the island. It's colourful scenery, and warm, clean sea air a world a way from the claustrophobic and heavy metal London existence she had left behind. Sally had always loved beautiful things - a new handbag, a designer dress, her chiselled husband - but she had almost forgotten the beauty that was really in the world - and this place was bringing it back to her.

Initially, she very much kept herself to herself. When she wandered around the island or across one of the beaches, the locals would smile and wave at her, or raise their sandy caps, or even shout a welcoming hello, which she enjoyed, but she rarely entered conversation.

She was enjoying herself, but she very much wanted to make small steps. She knew there were British people on the island, tourists, and perhaps in time she would look to make a few friends. For now, she was happy in the company of herself and the sand of the beaches and the heat of the sun.

Sally had made a conscious decision not to attempt any writing until she had cut down on the booze - which was still a prevalent part of her life in the first few days in The Seychelles. In the evening, she enjoyed the walk over to the local beach bar — *Vic's*.

She would trudge there at lunch time most days, order herself one of the many cocktails on the menu - her favourite was a *Long Island Ice Tea,* naturally, the one with the most booze in it, and set herself up in her favourite spot - under an umbrella furthest away from the bar itself, looking down the long thin beach.

She would take a book with her, she had bought a load with her, and it was when she was reading *Separated at Sea,* A tale of 17th century romance and piracy, that she first got the feeling that someone was watching her.

It was an uncomfortable feeling, it penetrated her internal happiness and made her feel paranoid. Whenever she looked around though, she saw nothing but patrons chatting away cheerfully over their beers and seafood. At first, she just put it down to paranoia, a lasting knock on effect from the anxiety she had been struggling with back at home.

The only person she really spoke to in the bar was the barman himself, a huge, very cheerful, african-american man named Vic. He was kind to Sally, and had picked up very quickly she was not looking for conversation. He would prepare her Long Island Ice Tea when he saw her approach, and hand it to her with a cheerful smile and occasionally ask how she was, or what she was reading. He would always diligently come over when he saw her glass was nearly empty, so she knew he must be watching occasionally.

But what she was feeling was more intense, more unsettling.

As time passed, the feeling came and went. The people around her in the bar where often varied, but there was a core group of patrons that seemed to be there from eight in the morning till closing time, drinking hard liquor. Sally did not let this feeling deter her from one of Vic's magical cocktails, in fact, it seemed to make her want to come back to the bar more and more, an internal sense of intrigue reeling her in.

Three weeks had passed, and Sally had grown used to it - and had in fact written it off. It was a particularly warm, humid afternoon, and Sally was reading *Girl Allergies*, a rather short little story of a boy who couldn't talk to a girl without getting itchy and sweaty, that a man approached her, and offered to buy her a drink.

He was a handsome man, that was for sure, he had long brown hair, tinted by the sun, and a perfectly kept stubble. His teeth were a gleaming white, and his shirt hung open, enough to show the muscle definition his chest hosted. Sally had already had a few Long Islands this afternoon, so she accepted.

He introduced himself as Kirk

Sally had forgotten that she did in fact like people, she had almost brainwashed herself into thinking that being on her own was better, when in fact the more she isolated, the more cut off from the world she was becoming, and that was hampering her creative abilities.

That afternoon she spent with Kirk, she did not think once about being watched.

CHAPTER 4

Kirk

One thing was for sure - Sally very much enjoyed spending time with this man. He was funny in a sarcastic way (Sally loved sarcasm), charming, and easy to talk to. Sally, of course, was not interested in him romantically, but she enjoyed his company none the less - talking to someone was far better than the long periods of silence she had put herself through.

Sally wondered if she was still attractive to men. She had begun to take a bit more care in her appearance again, she slapped a bit of make up on in the mornings - although she didn't really need it. She washed her hair most mornings, and her long blonde curls now glistened once again in the sun. She had lost a lot of weight back in London, she was not eating much - and the gin and tonics didn't exactly pile on the pounds.

She had eaten well since she had been in the Seychelles, and her figure was looking strong again. Sally was tall, and what she did not know is that sometimes she could be intimidating to men.

Kirk - however clearly had not been intimidated. As the sun set on the first afternoon they had spent together, Sally had taken her leave - and Kirk had asked if she would be returning. Sally told him she came here most days, and did not really have any friends, so she would be happy for him to keep her company if he was at a loose end.

She was not sure if that was a good idea, but after six Long Island Ice Teas, and a couple of shots, she was feeling particularly friendly.

Kirk had told her about his own family - he had a wife, called Sarah, a woman from Scotland who worked in the Seychelles, and a young boy, named Wayne - who was just old enough to spend the day at the local nursery. Sally did not like the name Wayne.

Sally had asked one day why, if they lived here, that he was never at work. Kirk, in a rather embarrassed manner, proceeded to tell Sally that he had received his money after the death of his Father - who had owned a lucrative tech business in Leeds.

Kirk had used the money to purchase a business in the Seychelles - it involved taking people out on the speedboats at the docks, and also activities like scuba diving and snorkling.

Kirk said the business came with a manager called Amari, who knew all the ins and outs, and Kirk said it was easier to leave the day to day running of the business to Amari - and therefore Kirk could enjoy himself in his new home. Kirk said his wife, Sarah, had picked up a job at the local Spa, she had felt a bit lost after Wayne had started at nursery, and had no intention of spending her days living a life of leisure just yet. Sally thought Kirk seemed to quite enjoy having the days as his own.

Kirk had taken Sally up on her offer, and returned most days in the afternoon, sometimes only briefly, sometimes for hours. They wiled away the afternoon drinking and talking about anything from their favourite reality TV show to the British foreign policy.

Sally wondered why Kirk's wife never came with him, particularly on the weekends, but believed him when he said that she did not really enjoy drinking - and imagined the little one was probably too young to spend entire afternoons on the beach.

One particularly boozy afternoon, Kirk had asked Sally if she would like to go out on a yacht cruise that they were putting on soon. They would be out on the water for a few days on a huge sun seeker that they had rented - Kirks wife and child would be joining them, as well as a number of other customers who had bought a ticket.

Sally was excited at the idea, and had told George over the phone that night. He had encouraged her to go ahead with it, she deserved to have some fun. He also, understandably, seemed a lot more relaxed about it when Sally told him that Kirk's family would be coming with them. She had not told him that she had this feeling that she was being watched, and the only time she did not feel it was when she was with him.

The day before the cruise was set to depart - Sally was back at the bar, Kirk had not come today, obviously busy with the last minute preparations, when Vic, came over to her, and with a grave look on his face, said more to her than he ever had before;

"Hey Miss Sally, you be careful around that man, whispers of him being a dangerous man, islanders scared of him - he come with his money, buy our local businesses. Last year, on one of his cruises, they came back without this man, vanished he did. You must be careful when you around him."

With that, Vic passed her another Long Island, which he signalled was on the house, and walked away, back to the increasingly busy bar.

CHAPTER 5

Questions

Sally had a couple more drinks, mulling over what Vic had just told her. She felt tense again for the first time - and the feeling she had of being watched returned swiftly. It unsettled her, but the drinks helped. They always helped.

Sally returned to her apartment as the sun began to set. She felt uncomfortable for the first time being on her own, but she was beginning to feel fuzzy and light headed. She wondered about Kirk. He had been nothing but good to her, a friend when she needed it. She liked him, perhaps more than she realised. Everything about spending time with him seemed dangerous and reckless.

She managed to stumble around the kitchen and make herself a sandwich. Sally had some cold chicken and some mayonnaise in the fridge. She did not particularly like the mayonnaise here, it was a bit sweet for her, but the alcohol masked the taste nicely. She poured herself one last glass of wine, and sat on her porch. She liked the darkness tonight, she felt concealed, hidden from dangers in the world. The silence was a blessing.

Sally lay in bed that night unable to sleep, she tossed and turned, and cursed the air conditioning as she sweated, dampening the sheets. So many things were on her mind, but the main thing was what Vic had told her. She would be defenceless out in the ocean if this man was dangerous, but surely his family would be a safety net. Unless they were in on his schemes?

She thought back to the times she had spent with him, the laughter, the fun, the ease at which she kept his company. But also the fact she had never met his family, that seemed strange to her, was he hiding them from her. Did he want more from her?

She wanted to clear her mind, and a hangover was beginning to take hold even before she had a chance to sleep. She felt rough, and the anxiety was growing inside her, the longer she lay with her eyes open. She tried to block out the thoughts with happier times; when she first met George, when her book was released. Eventually, Sally dropped off to sleep.

Sally lay on the beach, her breathing quick, the salty sweat all over her body, causing the sand to coat her skin. Her legs were covered In scars that rose up her body. She felt weak from the running, running away, she was always running away.

The man that followed her in the jungle was surely close by. The dark silhouette haunting her, her legs were beginning to struggle to escape him. His dark silhouette was a menace in the green jungle. She could see it every day and every night.

The sea in front of her was vast and open, the sun glimmering on the cool blue of the water. She longed for an escape, but it was hopeless, the island was isolated, forgotten.

The rustling behind her turned to footsteps. She held her breathe. The silhouette approached her, holding out its dark arm. She closed her eyes, and felt his callous hand close around her neck.

Sally screamed as she woke up with a jolt. She was panting, sweat pouring down her forehead. She looked down at her body, half expecting to see scars, and put her hand around her neck, dreading the feeling of the hand she had just felt in her dream.

Slowly, she began to calm down. She got out of her bed, the sheets now damp from her wet skin. She was spooked, and it took a few moments before she remembered she had to be at the marina soon. For the trip, the trip that took her out to sea with a group of people she did not know, and a potentially dangerous man.

She stepped out onto the porch, trying to force down a croissant she had purchased from the bakery the day before. She felt dizzy, an uncomfortable pain spreading in her head. She no longer wanted to be on her own, her dream last night had felt horribly real. The isolation began to worry her.

But she knew the only hope she had of company was on a boat, with a man who she had been warned to avoid.

She thought about calling George, telling him about what Vic had told her about this man, and also about her dream. She knew it would worry him though, and she knew he needed space as well. She finished her croissant, and decided the best place to collect her thoughts would be in the shower. She poured herself a glass of wine as well. She felt guilty about it, but she needed it. As she poured it, she noticed her hand was shaking.

CHAPTER 6

The Marina

Sally felt better after a wash and a drink. The hot water had felt comforting on her body, and the alcohol had calmed her down. She rarely had nightmares, and when she did, they were rarely as real and as haunting as the one she had last night.

She got dressed and sat down to do her makeup. She did not wear much, George had always encouraged her to go without, she was a natural beauty. Sally had started to take a bit more care of her image since she was in the Seychelles, as she hated the fact that she had begun looking so dishevelled in her isolation back at home.

She eventually decided that she would go on this cruise. The second glass of wine had helped, but also her sense of curiosity and adventure. She felt she would regret it if she did not know. On top of that, she desperately needed material to start writing again - and a cruise with dangerous undertones sounded like the perfect place to start.

She also had a feeling that Vic and the locals are against the likes of Kirk due to the fact that he is buying their businesses. The story could well be fabricated to make him look even worse. Local men often had strong feelings about their territory. Vic was probably no different.

Sally gathered her things, and composed a text to George, as she doubted they would have any signal on the cruise.

Hey babe, hope all good at home. Off on a cruise today - exciting! I doubt there will be any coverage out in the ocean,

so do not be alarmed if you don't hear from me for a few days. Hoping to get some ideas for a book! Love you. Sx

The text sent with a little whoosh, and Sally gathered together her possessions. She was excited now, she had Never actually been out on a boat before, except one of those big ferries that take people to France or the Isle of Wight. She had more or less forgotten about her nightmare now, and Vic's words of warning had been forced out of her head by the alcohol.

When she arrived at the marina, it was early afternoon and blazing hot. She was certain the taxi driver had turned off his air conditioning, as she was sweating profusely underneath her yellow wavy summer dress.

The boats were magnificent - and she wondered how much one would cost. They stretched all the way down the front of the marina, They were all beautifully clean, the sun reflecting off their sparkly white shells. They bobbed gently up and down in the azure sea. Many of them had people aboard, girls laughing and drinking in bikinis, men in linen shirts and Ray ban sunglasses draped around them, beers in their hands. They oozed wealth, and everybody aboard the yachts seemed so happy - it looked a good life. The sight made Sally excited, but also a tad nervous inside. It had been a long time since she had partied with anyone other than herself.

"Sally! You made it!" Shouted a voice further down the marina. It was Kirk. She smiled at him and headed over to him. What she guessed was his yacht lay over his shoulder, it was a bit smaller than some of the larger ones, but still majestic. It looked like it had three levels, and there were two men out sunbathing on the deck. This comforted her, she looked forward to meeting a few new people, she had been concerned it would be just her and Kirk on this trip.

Kirk gave Sally a hug, he looked great she thought. His long hair was washed and tied up in a bun, the blonde streaks glistening in the sun. His shirt hung tight and open around his muscles, his skin tanned and smooth. She almost found herself staring at his chest, but snapped herself out of it quickly.

"Hey Kirk, wow your boat is amazing! I can't wait to meet

your family as well."

"Thanks Sally, so glad you could make it, it's gonna be awesome. They can't wait to meet you either, they are just on their way, shouldn't be long now. Anyway, come aboard lets get you a drink. We have a cocktail maker with us! Should be able to knock you up a Long Island Ice Tea, and I will show you to your quarters."

Kirk lead her up the gangway onto the boat. She watched and followed as he strutted onto the deck, introducing her to the two men there. One was called Giles, a childhood friend of Kirks, who seemed friendly enough. The other man was a bit quieter, his name was Jean-Paul. He sounded French, and it was him who apparently was the designated cocktail maker. Both men were young, fit, and apparently had heaps of experience at sea. Sally wondered if any other women were coming.

Once she had a drink in her hand, which Jean-Paul had handed to her with no more than a grunt, Kirk showed her to her quarters, a small room which was little more than a cupboard with a small bed. She did not expect much more - but it suited her, it had a little fold down desk as well should she need to make any notes for her book. She also had her own bathroom she was told, the boys would share the other one.

She settled in out on the deck, trying out a new biking she had bought, it was sky blue with little star fish on it, and complimented her figure perfectly. She wanted to be careful not to get too drunk to quickly, but the boys were cheerfully making sure her glass was always full.

She enjoyed Giles' company, who cheerfully regaled her with tales of his childhood adventures with Kirk, who stepped in every now and again to call Giles out if a story was slightly exaggerated. Jean-Paul sat across from them, quietly sipping his drink. Sally wondered if he was an actual employee - or if Kirk had invited him simply for his ability to make a drink. Or if he was just quiet.

The hours past quickly, and Sally wondered when they were actually setting off, she was beginning to feel a bit pissed now, but she was enjoying herself.

It was at about 5 o clock that Kirk came out of the his quarters, looking a bit distressed, clutching his phone.

"Right guys, I'm afraid my family is not going to make it - Wayne is adamant he does not want to go. He gets seasick you see, so my wife is going to stay at home with him. So we are ready to set off now, if everyone is OK with that?"

"What a shame old boy, they will be missed. But yes, I am ready to press on, Jean-Paul, could you fix us another drink before you take the reins?" Said Giles. His face was red now, burnt a little, and flushed with alcohol.

Sally realised that Jean-Paul of course, was the captain of the ship.

Jean-Paul took his glass, and then took Sallys, and disappeared into the boats interior.

Kirk looked at Sally, she nodded. But Sally was nervous now.

Did the family even exist?

Vic's words returned to her head once again.

CHAPTER 7

The Eclipse

Sarah watched as the Seychelles and the Marina faded away into the distance, engulfed by the beautiful blue water and the crystal clear skies. Had she made a terrible decision? She could not help but feel trapped. She was on her own, with two men she did not now, and Kirk - who she had no idea whether or not to trust.

She had come here to escape that feeling of isolation, which had crept up on her again. But now she had never felt more isolated, more alone. She longed to go back to shore. Kirk had told her the ship was called *The Eclipse*, and she could feel a certain darkness, a danger.

Kirk came and joined her at the railings, he could sense the change in her. She had become reserved over the last few hours since he had told her his family was not coming.

"Sorry about Sarah, Sally. But hey, we can still have fun, I know it is annoying being stuck with a bunch of blokes but we can still have fun. Are you enjoying the cocktails? If you really want to go back, it is not too late to turn the boat around"

Sally thought about this for a moment. Now that the offer was on the table, it almost made her feel a bit more comfortable. She thought about her writing, about this adventure. She could not miss out. She looked at Kirk, and managed a grin.

"It's ok Kirk, I want to stay. The cocktails are great thank you, I reckon it's time for another one. I think I am ready to hear some more of Giles' stories."

Kirk laughed, and pulled her in for a hug. Sally felt his strong arms enclose around her body. She could not help but like it. Kirk took her glass and led her by the hand back to the others, handing Jean-Paul the glass on the way. It was not long before she had another drink in her hand.

They spent the rest of their first evening talking, laughing and drinking. It had been a beautiful night, the sky full of bright golden stars, the soft breeze gently rocking from side to side. The music from Kirk's speaker flooding the deck and then vanishing into the open sea.

Giles had been the first to go to bed, and Sally watched him stumble over the deck. His face blotchy and red, his white shirt now stained with spilt whisky. He would not feel his best tomorrow, Sally guessed. Jean-Paul stood up when Giles almost fell off the edge, and helped the man down to his quarters, muttering a curse under his breathe. Jean-Paul did not return, leaving Sally alone with Kirk.

"I better get off to bed, I want to try and get something written tomorrow morning. One more of these and I will not be getting out of my bed!," Sally said, shaking her empty glass at Kirk. She felt tired and full of booze, she did not think it was a good idea to stay out here just with Kirk.

Kirk stood up, the alcohol did not seem to have affected him at all. He took Sally's empty glass, and then picked up Giles' glass and Jean-Paul's, and turned back to her

"I think I ought to do the same, come on, I will walk you to your cabin. I'll wash these up before I go to bed. "

They made their way into *The Eclipse*, and Sally headed straight to her cabin. She thought about how she would love some company in her bed tonight, but she only wanted George, didn't she? The alcohol was clouding her mind.

"Sally there is something I have not been totally honest about," said Kirk, Sally turned and faced him. She was nervous to know what he was going to say next.

"Sarah and I, we are not doing great. In fact, um, we are getting a divorce. I am sorry I lied to yo, I just did not think you would come if you thought you would be the only girl. In all honestly I get the impression you need this as much as me. Sarah is gathering her things back on the island, she is going to fly home,

I could not bare to watch her go, so I decided to come out here. I am glad your here, I can't deal with bloody Giles's stories twenty four seven! If at any point you want to go back, just say the word, and we will go back. Anyway, good night, and I'm sorry. I will see you in the morning."

Kirk slid the door shut behind him, leaving Sally stood there, stunned. Should she go and talk to him, comfort him? He seemed remarkably OK for someone going through a divorce, but perhaps he was just putting it on. She decided against it, deciding she would talk to him about it tomorrow. She slid into her pyjamas, and settled into bed. The alcohol took her off to sleep straight away.

The next morning, Sally sat in front of her laptop. For the first time in a long time, words began to come to her. She felt clear and motivated. She documented her first few weeks at the island, and then her first day on the boat. She liked the fact that she did not know where this story was going.

At around lunchtime, satisfied with what she had achieved that morning, she headed onto the deck. The others were already drinking, and she was certainly ready to join them. Giles, who's sunglasses covered his bloodshot eyes, was not quite his usual self. Kirk looked at her, Sally sensed a vulnerability about him, since he had opened up to her, she smiled at him.

"Hey everyone, sorry I am late, I managed to get some bloody writing done! What a beautiful day, Jean-Paul, please can I get a drink? I'm ready to have some fun today!"

Jean-Paul grunted his usual grunt and scuttled off, and Sally went and joined Kirk by the rails. She gave him a hug, hoping it would comfort him. She looked out at the calm seas, she felt comfortable now. She wondered what was next in her story.

CHAPTER 8

Temptations

After some lunchtime drinks and a bite to eat (Jean-Paul had made up some sandwiches) things on the boat had died down a little bit. The sun and the booze had got to Giles, who had retired to his quarters early for a nap. Jean Paul headed back to the wheel, guiding *The Eclipse* gently through the ocean. Kirk lay on a deck chair, a soft snore emanating from his mouth. Sally, who only had two drinks at lunch, lay in her bikini, with a book in her hand, enjoying the peace and quiet.

She was reading *Writer's Block,* a pretty intense story, she thought, of a kid who needed to ace his English exam, but his surroundings in the exam room was making that a bit tricky. She resonated with it a little, it was one of a number of books she had bought with her. She still was not sure exactly how long they would be on this cruise for.

After a short while, Sally headed back into her quarters, to get out of the sun for a bit. She dozed in bed for a little bit, again enjoying the soft rocking of the boat. When she woke up, she decided to proof read what she had written earlier.

She switched on her laptop, but the screen was blank, where had her document gone? She scoured around a little, before giving up. Had she not saved it earlier? Had someone come in and deleted it? Kirk had been outside with her the whole time. Giles? Jean-Paul? She decided she had simply closed it without saving it, and cursed. She would re-write it tomorrow.

She got dressed, slapping on a bit of make-up, and headed

out to the deck. It was not long before she had forgotten about the mishap with her laptop. The drinks were flowing, Giles was seemingly resurrected, and Kirk seemed to be back to his old self. Jean-Paul had stayed behind the wheel, popping back every now and again to check on their drinks.

The sun went down late tonight, and the three of them ended up in much the same position as the night before. Giles got too drunk, and once again had to go to bed early. Another shirt ruined. Jean-Paul had not joined them, deciding instead to press on with their journey.

Sally decided that she would try and talk to Kirk about his divorce. She did not exactly press him for information, but it was not long before he was unloading it onto her. The alcohol triggering an emotion she had not seen before.

He told her about how he and Sarah had met when he was working in Dubai, and fallen in love instantly. They had travelled the world, seen everything a human could dream of seeing. Wayne had bought even more love into their life, but it soon stagnated. The last few years had been tough, and Sarah did not like the Seychelles. The arguments had got out of control, it didn't take long for him to be presented with divorce papers. It had, apparently, destroyed him, but he had got used to it now, and was ready to move on with his life. He spoke confidently, but Sally could sense an inner sadness, particularly when he had spoken about their wedding, a beautiful ceremony on a beach in Australia, surrounded by all their friends and family. He said it was the happiest he had ever been.

The drinks continued to flow as darkness descended on the boat. Sally told Kirk about her problems with George, and her self perceived fall from grace. Sally did not often release her feelings to people, but she felt comfortable with Kirk. She liked his company, more than she should. There was an atmosphere growing between them. She could feel them growing closer. It worried her.

It was getting late, and they were both drunk now. Sally told Kirk she was heading to bed, and once again he offered to walk her to her quarters. She did not stop him. This time he followed her, rather than leading, and when she got to her door she spun around. When she looked back at him she felt a lust, a desire for him. She tried to fight it, but it had well and truly ignited inside her.

Kirk thanked her for listening to him, and went to give her a kiss on the cheek. He felt it too, the sexual tension was reaching a climax. He pulled away from her cheek, and she stared deeply into his eyes. A magnet was pulling her towards him, but she did not fight it. She pressed her lips against his. He put his arm around her waist, pulled her closer. She could not stop herself, putting her arms around the back of his neck, her tongue now in his mouth. It was not long before they were in bed, their clothes on the floor.

They made love passionately, Sally wrapped herself around his muscly, smooth body. She had not had sex in months, it had taken her away from the world, given her the release she had craved. Her desire for him had taken over her body and her mind, and she gave herself to him. When the deed was done, Kirk held her for a bit in silence. The bed rocking gently from side to side with the boat. He left before she could fall asleep in his arms, kissing her one last time.

It was not long before she sobered up, and the euphoria wore off. The guilt hit her like a train. All she could think of was George. What had she done. She had given in to temptation. But she had loved it, loved every second of it, and all she wanted was Kirk back in her bed.

She lay there, completely lost in her thoughts. Just as the anxiety was reaching fever pitch, she heard a shout from the quarters next to her. It was Kirk. She froze as she heard the words.

"Sally! Jean-Paul! Come here! Come quick! It's Giles, he's... there's blood every- he's dead!!"

CHAPTER 9

Murder on *The Eclipse*

The scene in Giles' quarters was grim, and unlike anything Sally had ever seen before. It made the blood freeze in her veins, she did not want to look at the body but her eyes would not deviate. They were transfixed. Kirk stood by the bedside, his whole body shaking. His usual calm and strong demeanour completely absent.

Giles' corpse lay face up in the bed, his glassy eyes fixed in horror on whatever his last sighting had been. A large, deep cut across his throat. The blood, a horrifying dark shade of mahogany, had started to coagulate on the floor. There was no sign of rigour mortis however, he had been dead over half an hour but not much longer than that. Sally's skills as a detective did not stretch much further. Kirk had been in bed with Sally, It could not have been him surely. Where was Jean-Paul.

Sally crept over to Kirk. She felt sorry for the man, Giles had been his best friend. She wrapped her fingers into his hand. She was scared also, they were in the company of a killer.

"Where is Jean-Paul, he must have done this," Sally whispered into her ears.

Kirk looked at her, tears in his eyes, he tried to speak but nothing came out.

"Lets go and fInd him Kirk, come on. We should grab a knife or something from the galley on the way, he is clearly very dangerous."

Kirk nodded, and let go of her hand. They headed to the kitchen, going past Jean-Paul's closed door on the way. Sally had not been into the galley yet, it was small, but pristinely tidy. Jean-Paul had not produced much other than sandwiches and soup, and of course a lot of cocktails, but he had not left a grain of mess behind afterwards. It made her feel slightly uncomfortable. The man knew how to cover his tracks.

She thought back to how he had acted throughout the short trip so far. He had been quiet, unsociable, and generally seemed to dislike all three of them. Sally though he seemed a strange choice on Kirk's behalf, she made a mental note to ask Kirk about his choice to hire Jean-Paul.

She had wanted to know more about this mysterious man that was aboard the ship with them when she had first met him, but the chance to talk one to one had never arisen, and he did not seem like the sort of man who would want to reveal much about himself anyway.

Sally's head was pounding now, she had a tremendous amount of guilt bouncing around in her body after her exploits with Kirk, and she was also shocked that she found herself about to enter someone's room with a knife in her hand. But, she had never felt more alive than she did at this moment. If she ever made it out of here, she would have one hell of a story.

The two of them made their way slowly to Jean-Paul's door, and Sally pressed her ear against it. She had really taken the lead now, Kirk was in a trance. She could hear nothing.

She knocked, shouting his name. Nothing. She tried again, and did not even hear a stir. Her heartbeat quickened, perhaps he was elsewhere on the boat, hiding from them. There was no way he was off the boat, he had to be here.

Sally curled her fingers around the door handle, expecting it to be locked. It wasn't. Her heartbeat quickened, and she felt Kirk's heavy breathing on her shoulder. She felt more confident knowing he was behind her, even though he was a world away from the strong, confident man she had been having sex with only an hour ago.

She pushed the door open, but could see little, the room shrouded in darkness. She said his name one more time, but no movement. Her eyes adjusted as she fumbled for the light switch. She located it, and it clicked on.

The illuminating light stung her eyes, her hangover messing with her senses, but when she focused she could see a figure under the thin cotton duvet. It was not moving. She edged over to the bed, and shook Jean-Paul. Still nothing. She spun him over, dropping the knife with a scream as his empty dead eyes looked back at her.

Behind her, she heard Kirk catch his breathe and fall to the floor. The clatter of his knife, accompanied it. Jean-Pauls neck and face were covered in red blotches, and a black mark travelled around his neck. He had been strangled, and not long ago.

She looked back at Kirk. The only other person on this boat with her. Kirk was a murderer. But how could he have done this? She was with him all night?

Was there someone else on the boat with them. She picked up her knife, paralysed with fear, and moved past Kirk. She went back to her cabin, locking the door behind her.

She did not know what to do, she needed to get off this boat. What was happening? Who was doing this?

It had to be Kirk, didn't it? If it wasn't him, then she had surely left him to die. Who else could be on the boat? It was surely not big enough for someone to have been there undetected.

She slumped at her desk. Then she froze again when she saw what was in front of her. Her blood ran colder than it had ever been before.

On her laptop screen was a long, beautifully written script. It meticulously detailed the murders of Jean-Paul and Giles. The killer had been in her room, written on her laptop. She read on, her eyes glued to he

> *The girl, she was an easy kill, as she would naturally suspect it was Kirk. That asshole would also be completely useless in this situation, a good tan and a big boat does not make you strong. I would leave him until last. He will find the girl's dead body in the bed he had fucked her in. Then I will find him, and will slit his throat like his best friend. They will never find me. They don't even know where I am, or who I am.*

Sally read on, there was a note underneath the narrative of their deaths. It seemed to be addressed to her.

> *Sally, I hope you read this before your demise. I enjoyed reading your story of how you wound up here, but you are a much better writer than that, so I decided to get rid of it. You made a big mistake, I watched the barman try to warn you. You were stupid not to listen to him. You will die for it. Truth is, Kirk killed my brother on this very boat. I left a bottle of Rum in your cupboard, you may as well get drunk first, it's all you are good for. I will see you soon Sally. Enjoy your last moments.*

CHAPTER 10

Escaping *The Eclipse*

Sally stared at the screen, reading the words over and over again. They did not sink in. She would die in this very room, on that very bed. She opened her cupboard, and there it was, the bottle of rum. Sealed and full. It looked appealing, but she was sober now, and she wanted to keep her wits about her, the adrenaline was pumping through her body. She needed to do something, anything. She thought back to what Vic had told her about the man that had gone missing on this boat. Why had she not listened to him, she cursed her reckless decision, and then cursed again as she realised that she had left her knife in Jean-Paul's quarters. She did not want to leave her quarters, but she didn't not wish to die here either.

Sally sat for what seemed like hours. She had heard nothing outside her door, no movement, no sign of Kirk either. The sun was starting to rise now, the sun shining through her porthole. She gazed out, and that's when she saw it. Hope.

In the distance, she could see a small island, and a few seagulls. It looked far away, and very difficult to get too. But it seemed a better fate than death. She knew where the life jackets were.

She would try and grab one, silently. She would need to try and find Kirk as well, he did not deserve to die on this ship.

She clicked open the lock on her door, and peeked out. The corridor was dark and devoid of activity. At the end of the corridor to the left were the hooks with the life jackets. To the right were stairs leading down to the base of the ship, which is where the killer must be. She crept along to the left, and stopped at Jean-Paul's room. The door was still open, but Kirk was no longer there. Her knife was gone as well.

Sally weighed up her next move, should she try and find Kirk? If he truly had killed someone last time out, which she did not really feel he was capable of, then should she really take him with her. She assessed her options. She did not want to be stuck with him on an island, not after what happened between them last night, but she did not want to be alone, and she did not wish death on him either.

She returned to her room, and grabbed her backpack. She took out the clothes she had packed, and replaced it with the bottle of rum. She headed back to the kitchen , carefully not to make any noise. The boat still seemed lifeless, and the darkness was menacing. Had the killer cut the power as well? She reached for the light switch, clicked it. Nothing.

She opened the fridge, filling up her backpack with as much food as she could. She was fully aware of the possibility that she could die on this island, but she did not want to be killed here, by a murderer. She wrapped her phone up in clingfilm, and then put it in a sealed bag. She also grabbed a couple of bottles of water. She was ready to jump now. She would take a float, and hopefully paddle her way over to the island. She hoped she would be able to do it without being seen.

Before she left, she crept up to Kirk's bedroom, which was on the deck above. It was bigger than the others, with a double bed and an en suite bathroom. The door was locked. She called for him, careful not to be too loud. No response. Was he in there, already dead? Surely he could not be asleep, not after everything that had happened.

Suddenly she heard a bang below her, coming from below deck. She knew she had to get out of here. She muttered an apology to Kirk. If he was locked in there maybe he would be ok, hopefully he had one of the knives.

She silently descended the stairs, The noise down below was growing louder, and her pulse quickened. She crossed to the deck, which was littered with the glass from last night, a happier time. She put on the lifejacket, which wheezed into life, and put it on over the backpack straps. She said a prayer, and threw the rubber ring overboard. She looked back one last time, before breaking the water with a splash. She was sure the killer would have heard it, but doubted he would come in after her.

The water was warm, but suddenly the island looked so much further away. It was her only chance though. She started splashing towards it, the weight of her backpack was a hinderance but she knew she could not get rid of it. She had enough food in there to last her at least a week. The water was warm, the sun shining on her back. She could taste the salt, but did not allow herself to get tired.

She looked back at the ship after a short while. It was in the distance now but she still had good view of it.

On the deck was Kirk, and behind him a dark figure. Something at Kirk's throat glistened in the sun.

It was a knife.

She had seen the dark figure before. In her nightmares.

CHAPTER 11

The Island

George rolled over, his stare engaging Sally, his smile warming her. He laughed as he flopped his long arm across her chest, pulling her in close. Sally nestled her messy hair onto his chest, his soft breathing was soothing.

"I love you, Sal," he whispered into her ear.

Sally looked back at him, her hand running up and down his stomach, stroking his soft naked skin.

"I love you too," She said back to him. He grinned, and his head settled back onto the pillow.

They both lay there, silently blushing, brimming with love for each other. The air was clear, their lives were free. Their hearts felt full. Sally closed her eyes. She carried on brushing her fingers up and down his body, the touch of his skin was warm, welcoming. When she opened her eyes, her scream penetrated the silence.

The body she was stroking was not George. It was a dark silhouette.

Sally's eyes opened. She felt the sand all over her body, its grains irritating and sharp. She was covered in a salty sweat. Her clothes were wet, and her mouth dry. She longed for water, and she longed to be back in George's arms.

Then came the guilt, the memories of getting into bed with Kirk. She wondered if he was dead. She wondered if she would be stuck on this island forever. It's yellow beaches stood in front of a dense green jungle, it was vast, but would provide good cover. She would need to go into the jungle to find food. She had no doubt that she was alone on this island.

She looked out to sea, and the beautiful, majestic sunrise. The rays bounced off the water, and the sky was unburdened by cloud or rain. In other circumstances, it would have been one of the most amazing sights Sally had ever seen. Today, however she would not be able to enjoy it. Perhaps, she would not ever be able to enjoy it.

She had made it to the island with her last ounces of energy. The boat had not followed her, but sailed off into the distance. She had escaped death, but was this a fate worse than death?

Her backpack had made it with her, and in it she had the bottle of rum that the killer had left her, a few tins of food, and a solitary bottle of water. She took a swig of the water. Her lips cried out in glee as the dryness was washed away, the cool water shooting life back into her body. She was careful not to drink too much. She had no idea how she was going to survive, but she knew she could not drink sea water. It did not look like it rained particularly often here.

She had never felt this level of silence in her life - even though at times she had longed for it. Needed it. Tiny waves washed gently over the beach, some of them reaching her sandy toes. A soft breeze rustled the tall trees in the jungle behind her, and that was it. She felt there was nothing else. She was an alien to this land, an anomaly. She surely could not survive here.

She lay back down, allowing the memories of the last few days to penetrate her mind. The guilt ate away at her, but it was overcome with fear. She did not want to die. Not here, not on this spit of land in the middle of the ocean.

She grabbed the rum, and poured a little shot into the cap. She would make the bottle last, it would surely work quickly with no food inside her. She knocked back the small shot, it helped. Her body felt stronger because of the alcohol, her mind more resistant to her situation.

After a short while, when the heat became too punishing, she ventured into the outskirts of the jungle. Her mind was not at it's sharpest, she merely wanted to find some shade. It was easy enough to come by, the trees were skinny, but tightly packed, and the foliage at the top of their tall trunks quickly blocked out the sky. She felt the temperature on her dirty skin drop, the coolness refreshing. She found a patch of grass, the ground unburdened by humans, and lay down on it. It was not long before she dropped back off to sleep, the rustling of the leaves a welcome distraction from the thoughts circling in her troubled mind.

The pitter patter of rain began to fall onto Sally's body, gifting it's way through the foliage to the ground beneath. It quickly woke her, but she welcomed it. Her nightmares had been getting worse, and the cold water felt glorious on her skin. She opened her mouth, allowing the rain to fall into it.

She scrambled for her water bottle, and headed back out to the beach. It was nighttime now, and the air was cool. The bottle quickly filled to the brim as the rain grew harder. She had seen some coconuts in the jungle, and she gathered a few. She used what little strength she had to smash a few open, and set them down, allowing them to fill up with the rainwater.

She continued this routine for what seemed days and nights. It was not long before she ran out of food, but she found fruit in the jungle - coconuts, pineapples and mangos. She had managed to make her bottle of rum last for a few days, but it did not help her much. She needed to face up to her guilt, rather than run from it. Her affair haunted her every day.

Throughout the evenings, she had heard noises, a rustling in the bushes that was inconsistent with the breeze on the foliage. It haunted her, but she was unwilling to investigate. It was her curiosity that had landed her in this mess. She also thought the hunger and thirst had begun to play tricks on her mind. Madness was beginning to overcome her.

That was, however, until she saw it. The dark figure. It was watching her in the distance, crouched behind a bush. Sally tried to scream, but she did not have the energy. She was deep in the jungle, and she was not alone.

CHAPTER 12

The Dark Figure.

Sally watched as the figure moved closer to her, it was aware that she could see it. She longed for daylight, for some light to shine on this silhouette in front of her.

She summoned some energy once the shock had washed from her body, and she turned on her heels and ran. She could hear the figure following behind her. Just like her dream. She had seen this happen to her, but there was nothing she could do about it.

The darkness ahead of her was endless, fruitless. She sensed the figure getting closer to her. It seemed larger, stronger and quicker than her. She did not want to stop, to give in, but she was lost now. Thoughts crashed through her head, was she going to die?

The ground beneath her was littered with twigs and branches, as well as moss and roots, and it was not long before her foot tripped over one. Her head lurched forwards, and her body doubled over. She hit the ground with a crash, and then lay still, panting and panicking.

She felt no pain, the adrenaline pumping through her body had granted her partial immunity. The brief silence was penetrated by footsteps coming towards her. She tried to stand up, but her body would not allow it. Suddenly her ankle throbbed, and the pain came. It came like an explosion. Sally knew she was not going anywhere, and she started to sob.

Her situation had broken her. She had fled from her life and her great love, and then cheated on him. She had washed up on a deserted island, and she saw this as her punishment. She would be killed now, and she felt she deserved it. All she could think about was George. She longed for his embrace, one last time.

She held her breath as the footsteps got closer and closer, and she waited for the dark hand that she had seen in her dreams. She had accepted it now, she just hoped it would be quick and painless, she did not wish to fight.

The figure stopped behind her, but she did not look. She just stared in front, into the darkness. The hand came, she sensed it. But it did not go around her neck, it went on her shoulder, and then a voice spoke in her ear.

"I am not going to hurt you. I am stuck on this Godforsaken island as well. I saw you come in from the boat. Kirk's boat. I was once on that boat as well. I wanted to talk to you sooner but I did not wish to frighten you. What is your name?"

Sally absorbed the words, and then turned to look at the man. He was no longer a dark figure, she could make out his features. He was tall, but gaunt, skinny. His skin was dark and tanned, perhaps even burnt from the sun. His facial hair had grown long and scraggy. His eyes looked damaged, though she could not tell their colour in the dark of the night. His hand on her shoulder was rough and callous. His clothes were torn and dirty. They had once been a smart white shirt and some cargo shorts. Pain and sadness oozed out of the man, but she no longer feared him.

"I- I'm Sally, I thought I was alone. I, er, everybody on the boat was killed. There was a man on there with them. I had to escape. How long have you been here? What is your name?"

The man flinched slightly when Sally mentioned that another man had been on the boat. He removed his hand from her shoulder, and then knelt down next to her.

"My name is Thomas, though my friends used to call me Tommy. I fear the man on the boat was my brother. He knew that I had gone out with Kirk and he knew I had not returned. I am sorry you had to go through this."

Sally was shocked - this was the missing man that Vic had spoke about in the bar, the conversation seemed an age ago.

The two sat in silence for a short while, the noises of the jungle once again taking control. Sally wondered why Tommy had left the boat, if there had been no killer? She would ask another time. For now she was just happy to have company, something to take her mind off the horrible thoughts that had been consuming her.

When the pain subsided in Sally's ankle, Tommy helped her up - leading her through the dark jungle. He had said he had put together a little camp with a few things that had washed up on the beach. Much more than she had achieved, Sally thought,

After what seemed like an eternity, they made it. Tommy's 'camp,' was nothing particularly impressive. There was a tarp hung over a tree branch which provided shelter, and a ring of stones surrounded the charred remains of his previous night's fire. He had managed to find some sheets which he stuffed with leaves, and he motioned Sally to lie down on it. She did, and the softness on her back was welcoming.

She watched as Tommy started a fire, aggressively flicking some dry stones together, something she had previously only thought happened in the movies. She wondered if this was her life now. Stuck on an island with this man. She soon drifted off to sleep, the warmth of the fire easing her into her dreams.

CHAPTER 13

Tommy and Nick

For the days that followed, little conversation took place between Sally and Tommy. Sally's ankle made it difficult to walk, and with the only pain killer being the nearly empty bottle of rum - she was rarely in the mood for smalltalk. Tommy spent most of the daylight hours searching the island for fruit, or out on the beach. Sally thought it was strange how acclimatised to the island Tommy had become, it was almost as if he enjoyed being here.

After a few days, Sally was able to hobble around. The pain was gruelling, but she did not like having to lie on her bed of leaves for hours every day. All she had was her thoughts, her recent memories, and they were not pleasant. They were grinding her down. Soon she would give up, overcome with guilt.

She had resigned herself to her fate, but she still clung to life, although she was not sure why. Even if they were rescued, she would have to face her husband knowing what she had done. She also had no doubt that the memories of the corpses on *The Eclipse* would haunt her dreams forever. She had been marooned on this island, and left to die.

One evening, as the sun set in the red sky, Sally decided to engage Tommy, in order to try and take her mind away from her problems. He had no issue regaling her with his story as to how he ended up here. In fact, it seemed he welcomed an audience. This is Tommy's story.

Tommy had arrived in the Seychelles with his brother Nick, about 2 months before Sally. Nick had recently split from his wife, and it had not been pretty. Nick had been drinking a lot, and getting in various bar fights. He was one conviction away from jail time, when Tommy came up with a plan to get him away for a little while.

They had planned to travel to many different places, but the Seychelles had stalled them. Nick seemed calm here, infused with the beauty of the island. Tommy noticed a difference in him quickly, the anger seemed to diminish, and he even saw his brother smile a couple of times.

They decided to stay on at the island, renting an apartment with what they had saved for the rest of their adventures. They were both content with the decision. They spent a lot of time exploring the island - the food, the bars, the trails, and the women. Nick had always been a hit with the ladies, and it did not take long for him to refind his mojo. Tommy was more reserved, but he was happy his brother was putting his broken marriage to the back of his mind, one way or another.

Tommy had met Kirk whilst at Vic's, the same as Sally (Nick had been off somewhere with a girl that day). He had approached him and the two had got chatting - the drinks flowed. Kirk did not leave without inviting Tommy (and Nick, if he was available).

Nick did not fancy the trip, and prepared to continue prowling around the bars that day. Tommy headed off to the marina, where he met a very excited Kirk and boarded *The Eclipse*. Kirk's wife Sarah, and their son Wayne, as well as Giles and Jean-Paul, were all there.

Much like Sally's trip, it started out jolly, the drinks going down quickly under Kirk's leadership. However, one night when they were out at sea, it all went wrong.

Jean-Paul and Giles had gone to bed, a situation Sally knew well, when Tommy heard a commotion coming from the deck. He went out to investigate, and found Sarah crying, Kirk screaming at her, his fists raise. His face had totally changed, there was so much anger, he was ready to hit her.

Tommy tried to get involved, help the lady, but Kirk was a strong man, a powerful man. Tommy got in-between Kirk and his wife before he could strike her. But his bravery was rewarded with a fist to his face. Sarah managed to get away, screaming. But Kirk was not done there.

Tommy tried to defend himself, but Kirk was too strong for him. The man was totally overcome with rage. Tommy had never seen fire in the eyes like he saw in Kirk's that night. Not even in his brother. It horrified him.

Kirk beat him and beat him, and Tommy for a moment thought he was going to die. It was then he realised his only option. He had to go overboard. So he backed away to the side of the boat, and pushed his body over the railing, falling into the sea. His face was burning with pain, and the water turned red with his blood.

Tommy remembered very little after that, but he washed up here, on this island. The same as Sally. He imagined that everyone thought he had died. Nobody would come for him. His brother would be on his own. Only Nick knew that he had been on that boat - so when Kirk returned to the Seychelles, without Tommy, Nick must have decided to seek his own vengeance.

Sally watched Tommy tell his story in silence. Her jaw dropped when she heard about Kirk, about the violence inside the man, the man that she had let into her bed. It sent shivers down her spine. She was disgusted with herself.

Tommy was visibly shaken after telling his story, though he had told it quickly and efficiently. It is probably all he has had to think about whilst he has been here, Sally thought.

After the story, Tommy stretched out on the ground, and it was not long before he was asleep. Leaving Sally to stew once again in her thoughts. She reached for the rum and finished off the last gulps of the bottle. Her head began to spin, she had no resistance to the alcohol anymore. She liked that, but now the empty bottle would add to her anxiety.

CHAPTER 14

The Chocolate Wrapper

As the fruitless time on the island passed, the hot days became longer, and the mild nights became darker. Tommy was a quiet companion, out all hours of the day, gathering fruit and exploring the island. Sally's ankle was better now, but she was shocked to discover that she preferred being alone during the daylight hours, rather than stuck with Tommy all day.

In the evenings they spoke occasionally of their past, but Sally did no tell Tommy the truth. She did not know why, but she did not want Tommy to know anything about her. She was ashamed of herself, drowning in a sea of self pity and guilt.

At least on this island, she could be whoever she wanted to be, and she would die here, die the person that she had conjured up.

The more she acted as this person, the more she believed that she had become this person.

She had been born in the countryside in the UK - a farmers daughter. She had various boyfriends before and during heading to Bristol for university, where she studied law. Her studies had narrowed her mind, she explained, and she lost touch with the outside world. She had various one night stands and flings, but she had decided that her job, when she became a fully licensed lawyer, had not given her time to have a boyfriend.

She had grown sick of being cooped up in an office, and the busy life in London (partly true), so decided to take this trip, to try and see a bit more of the world, to try and 'find herself,' as her few friends would say. The 'few friends' bit, sadly, was also true.

The more she told the story, added little bits to it, the more she accepted it as her true life. Perhaps it was the heat, or the hunger, but she could swear that memories of this fake life were even beginning to form in her mind.

She often thought back to that conversation with Miranda, at *Moonlight* in London. She remembered the excitement she felt at the possibility of an adventure, how much she needed it. She would remember that day as the day she died, as without that day, she would not be here. She was sure she would die here.

Tommy was a good listener, rarely interjecting, and asking only questions which were manageable. They both knew they were going to die. She was worried at first that he might fancy her, maybe he would want some 'end of the world' sex, but Tommy did not seem interested at all. That pleased her, she did not wish to die with anymore guilt, anymore regrets.

Sally had lost track of how long they had been on the island, it felt like years, but in reality it had been a couple of months. She wondered what George must be going through, her sudden disappearance. Perhaps her book would get a surge of interest, now she had been on the news. People love reading dead peoples stuff, after all. She hoped he would find happiness again, take a wife that would give him kids, and give him the life he deserved.

Every now and again, Sally and Tommy would move their campsite. It was at least something to keep things fresh - find new sources of fruit, plus the ground would become charred from their fires each night.

The jungle seemed endless, Sally had not covered the whole of the island, not even close, but she knew there was nothing there except trees, greenery, and sand. It was a simple existence that served as her gateway to hell.

Sally wished her guilt could give her some time off, but it never relented. Her thoughts were clouded with the image of Kirk's naked body, the blurry memories of the night they spent together. Her isolation overloaded it into her subconscious brain.

She had given up.

One evening, however, as Sally and Tommy sat around the camp fire, she noticed something that would change everything.

Tommy had worn a pair of Timbaland boots, which were now

a light brown because of the sun and the sea water. The laces were frayed, and the stitching hung off them like cats whiskers. When Tommy took them off this night, Sally saw the fire illuminate something on the sole.

A wrapper, wrapper was stuck to the sole of his boots.

Sally squinted to make sure her tired eyes or the dancing fire were not playing tricks on her, but she was sure. It was a chocolate eclair wrapper, the sticky sweet must have attached itself to his foot. But where, how? They had shared everything they had with each other, and she was sure he did not have any chocolate. It looked fresh as well, the packaging was glistening in the light from the fire.

She did not say anything, but suddenly she did not trust Tommy. Did he have a secret stash somewhere that he was not sharing with her? What else did he have. Where was he going all day. She decided that tomorrow she would follow him. There was no point confronting him now, the only evidence she had was a sweet wrapper. It could have washed up on the shore for all she knew.

She felt a sort of internal madness at the fact a small chocolate wrapper had forced her to distrust this man, it had even scared her. Was the island doing this to her, causing an intense paranoia?

She lay on her sheet on top of the bed of leaves, pretending to be asleep. She heard Tommy follow suit, and it was not long before he was snoring. Who was this man. Tomorrow, she thought, she will have another adventure.

CHAPTER 15

Into the Jungle

Morning came, and Sally was ready for it. Her body, ravaged by a lack of food and drink, her hair dirty and dread locked, and her torso skinny and frail, felt injected by a sense of wonder. Today, for the first time in a long time, she had a purpose.

She watched as Tommy got up in his usual laboured fashion. They briefly exchanged pleasantries, before Tommy ate a mango, and put on his boots. Sally noticed that the wrapper was gone, disposed of. She hoped that she had not been seeing things the night before. Tommy took a sip from a water bottle which still had a little bit of rain water in it from a few days before.

"Feels cooler today, I might be able to get deeper into the jungle, bring back some more food for us. I'll see you later Sally," said Tommy, before turning and heading into the jungle, the rustle of the leaves quickly growing silent as he marched further away.

Sally bided her time, then sat up and started to follow him. Her ankle was sore, but the pain was covered by this new found sense of adrenaline. Even if this came to nothing, she would enjoy this sense of urgency whilst she could.

The first thing that Sally noticed is that Tommy seemed to be moving much better once he was out of sight. He had a bit of a limp when he was around her, but that seemed to have vanished, he covered the ground quickly and efficiently, and Sally was struggling to keep up, her body tired and drained.

After about an hour of trekking, Tommy stopped, and so did Sally's heart. Had he heard her? She had stepped on a few twigs, but nothing that she thought would give her away. She quickly hid behind a thin tree, which was just about wide enough to cover her ailing body. She watched as Tommy knelt down, pushing what looked like a pile of leaves out of the way.

Suddenly, a small back pack was in his hand. Sally felt the anger boil up inside her as she watched him pull out of it a full bottle of water, alongside a small pack of biscuits - the kind you get on a plane or in a hotel room. She thought about confronting him, but once Tommy had reburied the ruck sack, he pressed on, and Sally followed. Was there more?

Tommy was still moving quickly, he seemed fit, very fit. Too fit for someone that had been marooned on an island with barely any food or water. It had been an act.

They had gone much further than Sally had ever been in the jungle, and her body was starting to fail her. She knew she could not go back, as she would be lost. She gathered all the energy she had, and pressed on, hoping that soon Tommy would be getting to his destination. He clearly had a destination, as he had not stopped to check the trees for fruit. He knew where he was going.

After about three hours of walking, the jungle was coming to an end. She could see sand through the trees, and she watched as Tommy made his way out onto the beach. She waited a few seconds, then went to the edge of the tree-line, and observed him walk quickly across the sand.

Her jaw dropped when she saw where he was going.

Slightly out at sea, bopping in the water in all its glory, sat *The Eclipse.*

The white paint glistened, reflecting the sun. It lay still, peacefully masking the horrors that had gone on inside it. Sally watched as Tommy strolled into the sea, swimming quickly out to the ship. He climbed the ladder to the rear, then he was gone.

She knew she had to follow him. Everything he had told her had been a lie. She wondered if his brother was still here, if Kirk was still alive. When she was sure it was safe, she headed over to the edge of the water. She had barely been in the water since they had moved deeper into the jungle, but it felt good on her skin, the cool water cleansing her of the dirt she had accumulated. She wished she had a drink, to give her more courage. She would have to go without.

She pushed through the water as quietly as she could, and arrived at the base of the ladder. She pulled herself up, which required more energy than she had hoped. She climbed it, and then she was on the deck. It was deserted, the deck that had once been filled with Giles and Kirk's tales of past debauchery lay silent, almost haunting.

She stopped to think about what to do next, she decided that she needed some sort of weapon, for she did not know what she would find on the boat. Was Tommy's brother still on the boat, were they holding Kirk captive? She edged through the glass doors that led into the galley, and breathed a sigh of relief as she saw that it was empty. The galley still had all its equipment in place, and she wrapped her palm around one of the kitchen knives. It empowered her, she felt ready.

She made her way out of the other side of the Galley, and tried to listen. She could hear movement below deck, and she edged down the stairs. Her hand was shaking now, but she had forgotten how tired she was, the blood pumping quickly through her veins.

She walked past the cabins, including her own, and the two that probably still contained the dead bodies of Jean Paul and Giles.

She reached the thin staircase that led to the bottom deck, then she heard Tommy.

"...and if they don't pay up soon, you're going to be dead, and it's not going to be pretty...."

Sally froze. Was he talking to Kirk? She edged closer to the door, it was open. She peeked round, and there was Kirk. Tied to a chair, covered in dried blood. His face staring at the floor. Tommy stood over him, staring down at the miserable, shell of a man in front of him.

As she contemplated what to do, a sudden pain exploded out of the back of her head, and the world went dark.

CHAPTER 16

Paradise Lost

Sally opened her eyes.

She felt drowsy, and the back of her head was burning, the pain was like something she had never experienced before. She went to touch it with her hand, but found they were shackled behind her back, and she was sat on a wooden chair. The room was dark, the floor covered in empty food tins, beer bottles, and congealed blood. She could hear movement above, echoing down the stairs. The brothers.

"S-Sally, you're Alive?" Said a weak voice to her right. It was Kirk. He did not look much better than her. How had he survived this ordeal. They must be feeding him, but he looked frail, and covered in cuts and bruises. The once beautiful man was not there anymore, and Sally could do nothing but pity what was left of him.

"Kirk, thank god your alive, I thought.. I thought you were dead. Why are they doing this to us?" Asked Sally. Her mind was slowly coming back to her.

"They want my money, they will not let me go until my wife pays up. I will not let her do that to Wayne though, I will not destroy my family's future. They can kill me first. They were planning to do the same to you. But these men are sick. I've heard them talking, and they have been watching you since you landed. At Vic's, on your porch, even in town when you shop. They know you are an author."

Sally thought back to all the times she was being watched, she had been right. It sent a shiver down her spine.

"But why has Tommy been with me in the forest, why did they not just tie me up like you in the first place"

"I don't know, maybe they wanted to do it one at a time - more manageable. Or perhaps they did not have enough food on the boat for both of us, and needed some time to pass. One could stay with you on the island, and live off the food there. The one that was with you." Sally thought about this, and decided it made sense, but she was scared.

"The one that was with me, he said that you went mad, that you were going to hit your wife and that he was defending her. What happened Kirk, on that first trip."

Kirk looked at her, seemingly shocked at these accusations. "That is not what happened." He said firmly.

"He had been all over my wife. Things between us have not been good lately, but he was being forceful with her, making her feel uncomfortable. I tried to stop him, and then one night he went into her room. I heard Sarah scream so I came running in. I had no choice but to punch him, he went back to his room, angry, and the next day he was gone. He must have called his brother through the phone on the boat. Told him what happened, and then headed to a nearby island. I think he had been here to see if they could extort us, but he gave into temptation. Then his brother must have snuck on when we left with you."

"When you jumped off the boat, we headed around to the back of the island. The other brother-"

"Nick, his name is Nick," Sally interjected

"Ok Nick, he tied me up, and went off and found Tommy. Thats when Tommy went out to find you, make sure you did not go anywhere, not that you could. Anyway, he came back in the day time, to eat, and to help Nick try and get me to cave. But I have held strong. Sarah and Wayne will have left the Seychelles by now, but they do not know that, they will be safe."

Sally was shocked at the story, at the madness of it. She thought about the ship's phone, wondered if it would be letting off any kind of signal. But she did not have time to process it. The two brothers came through the door. They looked exceptionally menacing now, Tommy no longer needed to limp, which gave his entire aura an injection of terror. Nick, who she had not yet seen, was shorter than Tommy, but he was bulky, and his clothes were covered in blood. His dark, penetrating eyes riddled with horror. He snarled at them both, and Sally could have sworn he licked his lips. It was Tommy, however, that addressed them.

"Welcome to our little party, Sally, I'm sure you missed lover boy over here. I wonder what your husband would say. Thats right. We know all about your life, I did not enjoy listening to all those lies you told me on the island. Nick here is quite the writer as well, I'm sure you enjoyed the little edit he made to your latest story."

Nick's snarl grew wider, Sally found it hard to believe this man was capable of such beautiful English.

"We could not believe our luck when you got on the same boat as this man. Two payments for one job. Kirk, are you ready to call that bitch wife of yours, or shall I make the funeral arrangements for all three of you. We cannot be found here, we have switched off your transmitter. We will kill you and then head back and kill them both. It will not be a quick death"

Kirk simply shook his head, then looked at Sally, mouthing an apology. He knew it was his fault she was in this situation. He knew his family was safe, and he had resigned himself to death.

Tommy stepped forward, and smacked Kirk with the back of his hand. Nick laughed, clearly enjoying this.

"Sally, how are we going to get your money, would you prefer-"

All four of them froze, as the sound of movement above deck echoed down the steps.

CHAPTER 17

Below Deck

"Who the hells that, get up there Nicky, take this." Spat Tommy, as he crossed the room and pulled a knife out of the drawer. Sally was surprised they did not have guns. She supposed they did not think they would need them.

Nick edged up the stairs, the noise had grown quiet now. Sally and Kirk looked at each other, perhaps a bit of hope flickering between them. Had someone found them?

Nick disappeared from view, and the three of them held their breath.

"TOMMY, Its-" Nick shouted, before he suddenly went quiet, and then they heard a thud, which must have been his body hitting the floor.

Tommy swore, before grabbing another knife, and stood behind Kirk. He was rattled, his whole body shaking. He put his knife to Kirk's throat, and waited. Sally wanted to shout out to whoever was on the boat, but she could not risk gambling with Kirk's life.

She heard footsteps, and she was comforted to hear more than one set. Whoever had come had come in numbers, she would be saved, but at what cost?

The sound made it's way down the stairs, and her draw dropped as she saw Vic walk through the door, then it dropped even further when she saw who accompanied him - it was George.

Sally was speechless. She felt a tear roll down her cheek.

In Vic's hand was a pistol, an old military revolver, Sally thought. Tommy knelt down, and shifted over to behind Sally. He used her as a human shield, the cold steel of the blade emerging across her throat.

"Come any closer, and I swear to God I will cut her throat."

George's face filled with tension and anxiety, he clearly had not known what to expect. But he was here, he had come to save her. Sally did not have time right now to think about what she had done with the man to her right. Unbeknownst to her, this man was about to save her life.

Before anyone could say anything, Kirk rocked his chair, slamming into Tommy and knocking him to the side. Vic, alert to the situation, fired two shots. Sally closed her eyes, and screamed.

When she opened them, she saw blood running across the deck, and then she felt hands on her body, lifting her up, the zip ties being cut off her wrists. She could not process it, she was in shock.

She stood up, and looked down, and Tommy's eyes stared back at her, but they were dead. Two holes in his chest were spewing blood out of them. He was gone. It was over.

George held her, and she burst into tears, allowing herself to fall into his embrace. Neither of them said anything, it was Vic that broke the silence.

"Miss Sally, Miss Sally, are you OK, thank God we found you. We were about to give up!"

"It's OK babe, let's get you off this boat, let's get you home." George said. He looked at Kirk, who was struggling to get up, he was so weak now. Vic helped him up, giving him and a nod, and they slowly made their way above deck, and off the boat. Vic and George had come on a speedboat. They would be back soon. As they sped away, Sally watched as *The Eclipse* faded into the distance, becoming a speck in amongst the enormous blue ocean. She afforded one last look at the island, then turned away. They all sat in silence. Sally looked at Kirk, and then her husband, but she was too shocked to feel any guilt, too thankful to be alive.

When they got back to the Seychelles, it had been Vic who had told Sally the story of their rescue. George, naturally worried about his wife after not hearing from her for almost two weeks, rang the company with whom they booked the apartment. The lady reported back that Sally was not home, but that she had been spending a lot of time at Vic's bar, just down the beach. George eventually got hold of Vic, who had relayed his fears about her heading out with Kirk.

George decided to fly out, and headed straight to the bar, where he met Vic. Vic sympathised with the man, as he had grown fond of Sally, but he was worried about this man Kirk. The two of them discovered, through asking about at the marina, that he had a family, but that they had left the island. Sarah did, however provide some information about the route that Kirk took on his cruises, and about the man who had tried to rape her on the last trip, who had then disappeared.

George decided that he would go after them, and Vic said that he would go with him, so they chartered a speed boat, and headed out. Vic had decided against getting the police involved, as presumably he wanted to dish out some justice of his own. George was not against it, but they had both been convinced that Kirk had been involved somehow. They had been wrong about that, Kirk had been just as much a victim in this as Sally.

Kirk had decided to stay in the Seychelles, and ended up investing some money into Vic's bar, but only to become a silent partner. Vic appreciated this, and the improvements in the bar saw a surge in business.

Sally and George flew straight back to London upon their return. Sally had told George about her affair with Kirk almost immediately, she had decided that she could no longer live with the guilt. It would eat her up, especially after what she had been through. George, though angry, immediately saw a change in her, and decided that he would review their relationship when she was back at home. He did not want to be without her. It would take time, but he felt they could repair their relationship

She had not been herself, not for a long time, but she was determined to change that, to become the wife that he deserved. Perhaps, sometime down the line, their marriage could become the paradise it had once been.

EPILOGUE

Sally stared at her computer. She was finished, she thought. The novel was complete, finally the novel was ready. She looked at the photograph of George on her desk, and she smiled. She felt a great weight lift off her shoulders.

She thought about what to do now, most people would now have a drink, but not Sally, she had not had a drink since she returned home. She had devoted her time to her husband and to her career, but this time, she had ideas, she had experiences.

George had not mentioned Kirk since they had returned, and Sally had appreciated that. It had allowed them to move on. She had a new found love for him, and now they worked together seamlessly, enjoying their time together.

She still had nightmares about her experiences, but as time had passed, they had become less frequent. When she did wake up screaming, George had always been there to comfort her, to hold her tight, and that had made things easier. Much easier.

The most therapeutic thing for Sally, however, had been the writing. It had taken her a little bit of time to be able to confront what had happened, but it had given her an endless amount of material to write about. Once she had started, it had flowed, and she slowly started to believe she had her mojo back. The hardest part to write had been her passionate night with Kirk.

George did not mind her including this, however he told her he would never read it. A fair deal, she thought.

Sally picked up the phone.

"Hello, is that Sally," asked Cynthia, her publisher, with a hopeful tone in her voice.

"Hey Cynthia, yes it is! I think, I think I have finished. I'll send it over now."

"Great, have you got a title for us"

"Yes I have, it's called *Missing In Paradise.*"

The Unfaithful Banker

"Cheating is easy, try something hard like....
Being faithful"

- Daniel Engelbrecht

CHAPTER 1

The Perfect Life

Ben lived the perfect life, if the perfect life meant that you had money, had a family that loved you and rarely suspected you, and were incapable of feeling any kind of internal guilt when you decided the warm embrace of your beautiful partner was not quite enough.

Ben lived with his wife, Maria, whom he had been married to for a respectable 15 years, and their two kids. The eldest, Johnny, tended to prefer the confines of his bedroom, and his Playstation, although Ben had suspected that 14 year old Johnny had recently acquired his first girlfriend. Being a teenager he was keeping it on the down-low. These sort of things tended to interest Maria a little more than it did Ben.

The younger daughter, Iris, was entirely different. She was an extrovert, always bouncing around, smiling and laughing. She reminded Ben of a younger version of his wife - full of the joys of life.

Ben had met Maria at university, and being a man that usually gets what he wants, he set his sights on her. Ben had been doing economics, whereas Maria studied English Language and the art of creative writing - which Ben thought was a menial and pointless degree.

Their paths regularly crossed in the various smoking areas of the campus - Maria was a bit of a free spirit, she worked hard, and Ben soon discovered she also played hard. She had long curly blonde hair, and was usually found in her trusty pair of denim dungarees, talking with her friends about where they were going to go out tonight, and which authors were guys with a female pen name.

Ben had made his move shortly after they had met; he had been out with his flat mates, and had probably had one too many vodka red bulls. He saw Maria, the light of the club illuminating her in all her glory. She looked like an angel, the dance floor appeared to open up around her, like a spotlight shone on her. Ben wanted her, and that night, he got her.

They were inseparable during the rest of their time at uni - bonded by a deep love of each other. Ben was different back then, he was caring, loving, and pretty funny for a guy studying economics. He had a way with words and women, he made them feel at ease, something which would come back to haunt him later in life.

They got married when they came back from a year on the road after university - a big lavish ceremony paid for by Ben's late parents in the countryside. Their friends and families gathered around celebrating an everlasting love. Ben had thought his wife had looked incredible, but then again, Ben had also thought the bridesmaids had looked incredible. He loved Maria, but Ben knew deep down, he was growing bored of Maria.

Johnny was born, and Maria's dream of becoming a successful writer was slowly fading, whilst Ben had become a successful banker in London. They had moved out to the suburbs, purchasing a beautiful family home - which put the final nail in the coffin of Maria's free spirit.

She loved her children, and was now confined to the 4 walls of her dream prison. Ben was always home late, regularly at business dinners or even staying overnight in the flat that he had bought himself in London. The sex had well and truly dried up.

She drank a lot more these days, and Ben had noticed that she was now taking pills to help her get to sleep. He didn't question it, he liked the fact that she was usually passed out when he got home - she would never be able to know what time it was, or smell the scent of other women.

So really, Ben, in his mind, lived the perfect life, but Maria had no such luck. He was in control. Ben merely needed her to raise his children, of which he was losing interest in as well. Everything, however, was about to change.

CHAPTER 2

The New Girl

The sun beamed through the bathroom window of Ben's flat, illuminating his handsome face in his oversized mirror. He enjoyed looking at himself, he knew he was still good looking, and if he needed any proof he just had to look back into his bed at Kelly, or was it Steph? No, Steph was last week.

Whoever it was, they had woken up with a lust for Ben, and he had happily obliged. He loved morning sex, it gave him a spring in his step before work, stroked his ego perfectly into place.

He completed his usual morning routine - calling them a cab, giving them a fake number, and 'promising' that he will call them later. He did a workout (in front of the mirror, of course) and drank his fruit and spinach smoothie. He had done this every morning for almost 8 years now - his body was in great condition. He was, at least, a healthy scumbag.

He decided to get an Uber to work today. Usually he got the tube, but the other day he could have sworn that he had seen one of his past conquests sitting on the tube, watching him.

The Uber pulled up outside his building. It was tall and ugly, made out of glass and bang in the centre of Canary Wharf. Every time he arrived here it made him feel like he had made it, regardless of the fact that he had grown bored of his job years ago. It kept him away from his wife and kept money in his pocket, plus he liked wearing the suits, especially when he ventured to the bars after work.

As he approached the doors, he noticed a magazine stand

which he did not think he had seen before. His pulse quickened as he examined the woman selling the magazines. He could have sworn that it was the same woman he had seen on the tube. He thought about investigating, but thought better of it, chalking it down to a bit of a paranoia, and the fact that the woman in the tube had just been fresh in his mind.

Ben quickly forgot about the incident, as he strolled into the lift, his mind back on work. He rode the lift to the upper floors, where he was greeted by Mark - one of few people that were above Ben in the food chain at his bank. Naturally, that made Ben despise him.

"Morning Ben, Just to let you know that if you see a strange face about the place today, we have a new girl starting in your division today," Mark said, "Oh, and try and keep your hands off her," he added, hoping to make Ben laugh. He didn't.

Shortly after, Ben sat at his desk in his little sealed off glass cubicle. He had no family pictures on his desk, just a picture of him and his partner in crime Greg at a Hooters on a 'business trip' to America. The picture sat alongside a small trophy from when his team at work won a 5 a side football tournament two years. Naturally, Ben had seen himself as the star player.

He fired up his computer and sifted through the procession of daily emails, including one from Maria, marked at 7:03am. Ben smirked as he considered what he was doing with Kelly at 7:03am, then cursed as he saw what she wanted. Money for a new gardener.

The day went on as normal, Ben spent most of it day dreaming. He marked his little black book - which kept a list of all his past conquests, he felt he may have needed it one day. A lot of them were marked things like, 'girl from Olympia,' or 'older woman definitely on cocaine.' However, some of these poor souls were graced with real names, and Kelly had made that cut. He always kept their numbers, you know, just in case.

As the day was drawing to a close, Greg wandered into Ben's office. "Alright old man, were you at the flat last night," he said, with a wink. "You seen the new girl, she's a right sort, just transferred here from God knows where, gonna crack on see what she's at this weekend I reckon. No rest for the wicked ey Benny boi."

Ben laughed, and shamelessly filled in Greg on last nights antics, before deciding he needed to see this new girl for himself. He always liked a new target, although he tended to avoid woman from the work place, you never know who's wife or girlfriend they could be, and they often wanted more.

When Ben saw her he froze.

She was the girl on the tube, the girl on the magazine stand. Green eyes, chestnut brown hair. Ben was confident now that he had slept with her before. Was she stalking him?

"Excuse me," he said to her, a bit shakily, "have we, er, met before?"

She smiled at him, "I've only just moved here, my names Emma, what's your name? I'm afraid I don't recognise you at all! Perhaps our kids are at the same school, St Michaels?"

Ben's kids were not at that school, but she seemed pretty sure they had not met. Ben was spooked, he kept a bottle of whiskey in his desk, and poured himself a quick drink to calm himself down. He was just being paranoid.

Ben decided that later he would go back to his family, he did not feel up to womanising tonight.

CHAPTER 3

Paranoia

Ben's anxiety heightened throughout the journey home, he once again had opted for an Uber, costing him a small fortune out to the suburbs, he didn't care - he couldn't face the possibility of seeing that face yet again.

He spent the journey trying to remember when had slept with this woman, and vaguely remembered a night which must have been 5 or 6 years ago, he had met her at the bar closest to his work, 'Olympia,' and taken her to his flat, he can't have had that much to drink if he could remember it. Maybe they had skipped the shots.

Ben arrived home, and he had not been this pleased to see his wife in a long time, she made him feel safe and at ease again. He poured himself a drink.

Maria looked good today, Ben thought. She had a red summer dress on, and a nice bronze tan. Her hair was as curly and voluptuous as ever. He had not noticed her in a while, oblivious now to her charms. The spark in their relationship had gone, but they were still civil.

Maria was pouring them a glass of wine each, wondering why Ben seemed so strange today, when Iris came bouncing in, over the moon to see her Dad.

"Daaaad!" She shouted, and ran over into his embrace. His family was giving him warmth today he had not felt in a while. Was he beginning to feel a little bit guilty?

"Iris had dress up day at school yesterday Ben, she went as

a minion, you know from that *Disney* film? Go on darling show Daddy your school picture."

Iris ran to her bedroom and returned with her tablet. It was actually Ben's old iPad, he remembered the sigh of relief he breathed when he remember to format it before handing it down to his daughter.

She got up the picture of her class. There was Iris, looking cheerful next to her best friend Lizzie, they had both gone as Minions. There were various other characters that Ben knew - Jack Sparrow, Harry Potter, even a Chewbacca, and a couple that he didn't.

His blood suddenly ran cold when he saw the teacher. His mouth dropped open. There she was. The same woman. Green eyes, Chestnut brown hair.

"What's your teacher called, Iris?" Ben asked, when he managed to slow down his heartbeat.

"Oh thats our new teaching assistant! She's called Miss Prince, she's new, we all really like her! She sneaks in a packet of crisps for us each on Friday's. Do you like my costume."

Ben's mind had left the room. Maria looked at him, confused.

"Thats funny," Maria said, "our new gardener is called Gail Prince, I haven't actually met her yet, she starts tomorrow. Thanks for sending that money by the way. What do you think of her costume anyway, pretty cool right?"

Ben dropped his glass, the crimson wine congealing all over the carpet. He left the room, Maria and Iris looking puzzled.

Ben could not tell Maria, obviously, that he was potentially being stalked by someone he had a one night stand with, but he was sure of it now, this woman was haunting him, and had gone to extreme measures to do it.

He spent the rest of the evening in his office, wondering what to do. He decided that he would go to work tomorrow and confront this Emma, what else could he do? He would also check his black book - maybe if he called the number at work, Emma would answer, he could watch her, and he would have his answer.

He eventually crawled into bed, he had drunk more wine than he had intended, hoping it would help him sleep. Maria was already fast asleep, breathing steadily, her open bottle of pills on the bed side table, next to a picture of their family.

Ben could not sleep, the anxiety and paranoia haunting him. The bulletproof man felt guilt like he had never felt before.

CHAPTER 4

Miss Prince

As Ben pulled away from home in his Uber, he watched out the window as the gardener arrived, and there she was again. Green eyes, chestnut brown hair. Ben gulped as she stared at him.

He arrived at work, sleep deprived and dishevelled, and went straight to his cubicle, pouring himself a glass of whisky. He peeped through the door, and there she was - Emma the new girl. How was she here, but also doing his garden?

He didn't look up when Greg walked in. "You alright mate, not looking too hot today, somebody keep you up last night?" Greg caught sight of the whisky glass hidden behind Ben's laptop, but decided not to say anything, and let himself out of the cubicle. Ben watched as he went over to Emma, she looked like she was enjoying whatever they were talking about, and his heart stopped as she glanced over at him.

Ben flipped through his black book, but couldn't find a Prince, or an Emma, but there were hundreds of spurious names and numbers around the time he thought it was, calling all the numbers would be hopeless.

He had to go and talk to this woman, find out what was going on, find out how she was in so many places at once. He felt sick at the prospect of it, about his private life being blown open to the whole world. He did not want to lose his family, his credibility and his reputation.

He went to the toilet, wretching loudly, when he felt it. The cold steel on the back of his neck.

"Hello Ben, remember me? You don't look too good there."

The voice was soft, but sinister. Ben was shaking like he had never shaken before.

"I want you to go outside the building, there is a van waiting, behind the magazine stand. Go and get in it, right now, or your family dies. I will meet you there." With that, the coldness on the back of his neck subsided, and he heard a door close behind him.

Ben thought about running, but he couldn't risk his kids getting killed. He was breaking inside.

The van was where Emma had said, behind the now deserted magazine stand. He wasn't sure if he was supposed to get into the front or the back, so he tried the front passenger seat, it was open, so he gingerly got in.

Shortly after, she got in the drivers seat, raising her jumper to show him her weapon. He dare not try anything.

She drove them in silence, finally arriving around the back of a block of flats.

"Flat 4b, 3rd floor, get going."

Ben walked into the building, his heart pounding, she followed close behind. She clicked open the lock, drawing the weapon as she entered the dark flat, and ushered Ben onto the sofa.

Ben looked in horror. On the wall there were hundreds of pictures of him and his family. Him with other women, Iris at school, his wife on the porch with a glass of wine. He had been watched for a long time.

"W-w-whats going on, why are you doing this?" Ben stuttered.

Emma went into her back pocket, and pulled out Ben's little black book, and threw it at his feet.

"You probably recognise me, but I am not who you think I am. 7 years ago, you slept with my sister. I am one of three sisters you see, triplets. Our other sister, Gail, is at your house right now, your new gardener. She is armed, and she also has a part time job as a teaching assistant at your daughters school."

"Our third sister, the one you slept with, is called Bella. After you had your little night with her, she got pregnant. She tried to call you, but the little prick that you are, you gave her a false number, I'm sure you do that to all your mistresses."

"Bella and the child both died in childbirth, you stole our

sister from us and ruined our lives, and you did not even care. So we are going to ruin your life and take your family away from you."

'You have a choice - I can either put a bullet between your eyes right now, or you are going to call your wife, right now, and tell her everything. We are also going to show her your little book of sin and all the disgusting pictures you have saved from your phone."

"After that, you're going to email your boss saying that you quit, and you are going to transfer me everything you have, and sign over your children's trust accounts, your home, and your flat to your wife. Her life does not deserve to be ruined. After that, you are going to get the hell out of London, and if you ever come back, I will kill you, and your family. Understood?"

Ben was numb in the body, and then he finally threw up. His whole life was ruined, he knew it. It was all his fault. He considered taking the bullet, but he was too afraid to die. A coward.

Emma passed a laptop to Ben, along with details on a piece of paper, and watched as Ben, in tears now, transferred everything he owned over to her. She had reduced him to a shell. Destroyed him just as he had destroyed her family.

Satisfied with the transfer, she got her phone out and dialled a number.

"Hello Maria…"

Seperated at Sea

"I think pirates, like astronauts, particularly for a boy, are always kind of worth thinking about."

- Daniel Handler

CHAPTER 1

ARTHUR AND MARY

The winter rain had hammered into the deck of HMS Harwich all the way home. The sea had not been kind to the sailors, huge, terrifying waves crashing into the side of the ship. The dark winter nights full of freezing cold air.

This night was no different, but Arthur was luckier than his crew-mates. Arthur had his wife, Mary to keep him warm at night, to hold his head up when he was sick over the side (he had managed both starboard and port, many times), and to keep him company through the long, sleepless nights.

Arthur and Mary had met in Boston on Arthur's latest trip. Arthur had spent two years in America, working in the busy shipyards of Boston, achieving, what he thought was very little. He had longed to return to England, but the opportunity had failed to arise.

Increased piracy had made the seas a treacherous place, and with no family to go home to, Arthur had decided to stick it out in Boston. His efforts had, eventually, been rewarded.

Arthur had met Mary in one of the many Irish pubs that littered the streets of his new home. He had immediately been drawn to her sandy blonde curly hair, her green eyes that looked the colour of a shamrock, her gleaming pearly whites that stood out amongst the dirt of the other sailors, and her ability to dance on a table no matter how much ale she had consumed.

It had taken him a long time too pluck up the courage to talk to Mary, she was always surrounded by drunken sailors, fascinated by her tales of growing up in Ireland, and cheering her on as she danced through the night. She was a popular girl, although none of his friends had ever been successful with her. Arthur liked this. His friends did not.

Arthur, on the other hand, was a shy man. He had spent his life on ships with his late father who had made sure that Arthur always put his job first. He had seen many a sailor get drunk and get into fights, jeopardising their future and the safety of their crew-mates. Arthur's father did not drink. Arthur, on the other hand, enjoyed an ale, he felt it helped him sleep, however he never got truly pissed like his friends. Arthur, for better or worse, enjoyed a simple life, but what he had desired more than anything was a companion.

Arthur remembered the warm summer night last year he had finally plucked up the courage to talk to Mary. He had decided to have one more ale than usually, trying to achieve what his Irish friends had referred to as 'Dutch Courage.' The pub was busier than ever, music and laughter bounced around the claustrophobic walls of the building, packed to the brim with red faced workers, newly docked sailors, half naked women and even the odd drunken child. Beer soaked the dirty wooden floor, and to be honest, the stench, to a sober man, was horrendous. Luckily, no one was sober.

Arthur had approached Mary, his memory a bit patchy given the extra drink he had allowed himself, but he had remembered her asking one thing, "Hello there old man, what took ya s'long!"

As it transpired, Mary had been aware of Arthur for a while, she had thought he was handsome, and above all was curious of him. None of the other men that drank at *The Squealing Pig* were like him, and Mary liked this. He was quiet and calm, and remarkably cleaner than the other men. Perhaps, she had thought, he had a bath more than once a week?

The two of them had spent the rest of the night chatting away, the other men regularly looking over, confused by the fact their dancing girl had possibly been tamed. That night Mary had come back to Arthur's cabin, and they had made love in the flickering candlelight, twice.

Mary never went back to someones cabin. Arthur was in love.

Everything since then had been perfect. Mary had married Arthur, and was to come home with him. This had led them to the HMS Harwich. Captain Lewis, had been more than happy to cater for them, once Arthur had thrust a few coins in his hand. He wanted to be home for the turn of the century. 1700, a new home, a new wife and a new start.

Arthur and Mary, however, were unaware that there was a threat greater than the harrowing wind and thumping waves, and it was quickly approaching the ship through the stormy winter night.

CHAPTER 2

HEARTBREAK

"PIIIRAAATTTEESSSSSS," Screamed one of the deck hands. Arthur, who had been dozing, not fully asleep, bolted up, his heart suddenly racing. He looked over at Mary, who was still snoring away, her arm drooped over the side of the bed. Arthur shook her until her green eyes turned to meet his, she could immediately see the fear in his eyes.

Quickly, she became aware of the screaming and running around outside their cabin. Arthur was not a fighter, he had never been trained in any sort of combat. The HMS Harwich had a number of soldiers on board, but they were weary and tired from the long journey, and had no doubt indulged in some drinks hours ago in an attempt to get a better nights sleep. Their wits would not be about them.

Arthur held Mary close, telling her it was going to be alright, when in fact he had no idea. He could see the anxiety had taken over her body, she was usually so free, so friendly, but now she was terrified. Arthur did not know what to do, if he was to die, he wished to die beside Mary, the love of his life.

Arthur got out of bed, and frantically pulled on his breeches and his boots. He found his ragged shirt on the floor, and threw it over his head. He caught a glimpse of himself in their makeshift mirror, he was white as a sheet. He chucked Mary her dress, but she was frozen with fear, and it came to rest on the bed.

She snapped out of it seconds later, and quickly put it on her. Arthur watched, would this be the last time he would see her beautiful naked body? With that he grabbed her cheeks and gave her a big kiss, before turning towards the door.

He turned the key in the lock (they kept it locked as Mary was the only woman on the ship, and the sailors tended to get a bit jealous when they had had a few drinks) and peeked out the door into the corridor of the crew quarters.

He held his palm up to Mary, telling her to stay in the cabin, and shut the door behind him, locking the entrance and placing the key in his pocket. He crept up the corridor, the ship swaying side to side with the extra weight on it. The double doors to the deck were in front of him, screams coming from the other side.

Arthur pushed the door slightly ajar, and looked out at the horror unfolding on the deck. The rain water ran red with the blood of his fellow sailors, bodies littered both sides of the deck as the pirates celebrated in a language he did not know. A few of his crew mates were on their knees with their heads bowed, shackles on their wrists behind their backs. The ones that had chosen to fight had been killed.

One of the pirates, a huge man with dark eyes, thick dreadlocks, a long scraggy beard and a faded brown leather coat, quickly spotted Arthur, and Arthur cursed. Surely it was over.

Arthur attempted to retreat, but the pirate was on him quickly, grabbing him by the ear and throwing him onto the wet red deck. The pirate searched Arthur, and his heart sank as the terrifying man pulled his blood soaked hands out of his pocket, holding the cabin key.

The pirate grunted something to a group of his comrades and they grabbed the key and made their way deeper into the ship. Arthur looked around, it was a miserable scene. The rain splashing off the backs of his dead crew-mates, pirates stood around their bodies laughing and swigging the ale they had looted from the deck. Captain Lewis' corpse lay face down at the far end of the ship, a crimson red river running from his torso. Arthur looked at the shaking man to his right, who's name he did not know. He was crying, and Arthur quickly realised that the man had wet himself.

The pirates started loading their prisoners onto their ship, and soon it was Arthurs turn. As they picked him up by his shoulders, Arthur watched the doors of the crews quarters as they swung open, the villains emerging holding a beautiful, aghast blonde woman. Mary.

CHAPTER 3

CAPTIVE

Drip, Drip, Drip

For many days, which could have been weeks, or months, that is the only sound that Arthur heard. The pirate ship was a lonely place, he had had various cellmates, but they had all killed themselves after the first night. Arthur could not do that, not without knowing what fate had befallen Mary.

Corpses of the men who had chosen to kill themselves remained in Arthur's cell for days after. The stench was unbearable, and the rotting flesh had attracted rats throughout the long bleak nights. He had strangely come to see them as companions in his isolation.

Madness was close, Arthur could feel that, but he had kept his head through memories of those nights in Boston with Mary. Once the corpses had been removed, the rats moved to another cell, only returning when a new victim was thrown into Arthur's cage.

Drip, Drip,

Arthur had searched the cell countless times for a way out, it had been fruitless, every-time. The pirates had been feeding him with leftovers from their meals, and whilst the food at first had been horrendous, he now welcomed it. He wondered why they kept him alive, if this could be called alive, what purpose he had in life. They did not put him to work on the ship, or ask him to fight when they raided other ships.

Arthur was still wearing the same clothes he had thrown on that night on the HMS Harwich, and they were now wet and rotten. His beard had grown and his hair thickened. He was practically unrecognisable from the man who had kissed his wife one last time. The memories of that night haunted him.

Drip

Arthur longed for hope, clinging on to the idea that his wife was alive. He had been a good prisoner, never attempted to escape or fight whichever pirate had given him his rations, and he dreamed one day at least maybe they would let him up onto the deck. He had become weaker, his bones clearly visible under his dirty skin. He closed his eyes, content that he would soon be in one his vivd dreams about Mary.

Drip, Drip, Drip

For many days, which could have been weeks, or months, that is the only sound that Mary had heard. She was sure when she was captured that she would be raped. But, thankfully, that had not happened. She could not speak to the pirates, they spoke another language, but they had fed her leftovers, like Arthur, and even gave her water in the morning each day.

She, unlike Arthur, had a small window in her cabin. She spent her days watching the now calm blue sea, dreaming of seeing another ship on the horizon. She had watched as the pirates had raided other transports, burning them after sacking them and leaving them to sink to a watery grave.

Mary did not regret leaving Boston with Arthur, she loved him more than she had ever loved anyone before. She had been excited about her new life, had dreamed about bearing her husband a child. She cried every night, as she was sure that this dream had been snatched from her.

Drip, Drip,

Mary was aware of how much weight she had lost, and wondered if Arthur would still fancy her if he was still alive. She, like Arthur, had kept herself alive with hope that she would see him again. She knew the life they could have together was worth waiting for, even in these horrendous conditions. She did not have a rat problem, she was higher up the ship, above the water line. That was fortunate, as Mary could not stand rats like Arthur could.

Mary's dreams were not warm ones like Arthur's, her mind

at night became clouded with horrible nightmares, flashbacks to the day of her capture. The memory of Arthur kissing her one last time as she pulled on her dress made her sad, and fuelled her tears, she didn't even know if he was alive. She was afraid of sleep, but tonight it came, like every other night.

Drip

Mary awoke to a bang. That was unusual, she rushed over to the window, her tired body injected with adrenaline. A huge ship quickly blocked the window, she did not see much but the men wore uniforms that she recognised from her time aboard the HMS Harwich; British soldiers. The ship had come to a halt, and she could hear shouting above her. The sound of hope suddenly overcame everything else, including the drips.

CHAPTER 4

Declan

Arthur heard the bang, which was too far away to hear the ensuing commotion. The ship had rocked to the side after the deafening noise, and Arthur was sure that the ship had been struck to the side.

The British ship had stormed the pirate ship, and cut down the pirates quickly and effectively. The pirates had been at sea for months now, and were hungry and tired, the menacing persona they created much less effective.

Mary had been found quickly, and she had been given blankets and food and a stiff glass of Ale. The sailors had been amazed that the woman had survived untouched in the ship for so long, she could barely speak, her curly blonde hair coated in dirt and her eyes filled with tears. If they had met the Mary from Boston, they would not believe the woman in front of them was her.

She said one word, 'Arthur.' She repeated it, repeated it like the drips that fell from the rickety ceiling of the decaying ship.

The soldiers felt for the woman, and quickly had her transported back to their cruiser. Mary watched with horror as the soldiers prepared to burn the ship, and rid the seas of the horrors that came with it. She grabbed the closest soldier to her - a young, Irish lad named Declan, his hair curly like hers had once been.

He looked into her eyes as she repeated the words 'Arthur,' but could not understand what this crazy woman wanted. Gathering all her strength, Mary managed to point to the bottom of the ship, as another tear fell down her gaunt cheek.

Declan, sympathising with the strange woman, leaped onto the ship, which was now ablaze, and ran into the galley, past his confused comrades, now convinced that another man, named Arthur, was aboard the ship.

Arthur, who's malnourishment had now rendered him unable to stand, could have sworn that he could hear a boy calling out to him. He could also have sworn that he was beginning to feel warmer.

The sound had become more clear, and now Arthur was sure. Whoever was shouting was getting closer, calling his name. Arthur crawled towards the door, as far as his shackles and his broken body would allow him, and started banging on the door.

Declan was beginning to give up hope, the smoke clogging his lungs as he rushed around the bottom of the ship, sweat pouring off his face now as the fire began to travel down the ship, picking up momentum. Old beams toppling to the ground around him. There were doors everywhere, and Declan did not have time to check all of them.

Suddenly, he heard a banging against one of the doors, and thanked god as he saw that it was an outside latch rather than a key. Holding his hand over his mouth he grabbed the rusty latch and pushed It to the side, opening the door which allowed smoke to pour in.

Arthur watched as the door fly open, and saw a short looking figure emerge through the smoke. A hand wrapped around his arm, the skin felt warm and young. He was soon hoisted up onto the boys shoulders. His weakness clearly an advantage at this time, as the boy was able to pick him up easily.

The ship was collapsing around them both, cut looked at the floor, the glassy, dead eyes of his captors staring back at him. Arthur wanted to spit on them, but his mouth was too dry.

Mary watched as Declan emerged from the ships galley, and her heart leaped as she saw that he had a body slung over his shoulders. The body of her husband. Declan came aboard the British ship just as the pirate ship spluttered and sunk into the ocean.

He placed Arthur on the ground next to Mary, she saw he was breathing, and she slid off her chair and lay next to him. Her tears now tears of joy. Arthur looked at her, as unrecognisable as he was, Mary knew he was still in there. The pair of them smiled at each other, and drifted off to sleep once again in each others company....

EPILOGUE

Arthur sat on his creaky rocking chair on the porch of his home at the Liverpool docks, and ran his hand through his clean, brown hair as he looked pensively out at the ghostly sea. He sipped at his ale, and breathed in the hearty smell of Mary's cooking. Tonight was lamb, Arthur loved lamb.

He stood up, and walked inside. He watched his wife, the most beautiful person he had ever seen, pitter patter around the kitchen, he always thought she looked so graceful, and tonight was no different.

Mary caught sight of him, and smiled at him, a smile that still to this day, melted Arthur's heart. He thanked God everyday that he had more time with Mary, the woman of his dreams. They had been to hell together, and now, he felt like he lived in paradise.

He put his arms around her waist and she giggled, and turned her neck to kiss him, he span her round, and stared at her, her face full of life again, oozing loveliness. His arm slipped mischievously down her back, he was still entranced her her.

Mary laughed, "Stop it Arthur, the boy will be coming down for dinner any second."

Arthur winked at her, "Well, it's about time young Declan knew where he came from."

The two of them laughed again. Happiness had found them. A new home, a new life.

Silence and Mist
A Post Apocalyptic Story

"I watched a snail crawl along the edge of a straight razor. That's my dream. That's my nightmare. Crawling, slithering, along the edge of a straight razor and surviving"

- Marlon Brando

PART 1

CHAPTER 1

Underground

It had been three years since the bombs had dropped. It had been three years since I had spoke to another human being or felt the touch of a woman. It had been three years since I had seen the sunset or the moon rise. Life had become the bunker, solitary and claustrophobic. But I was alive, and with life came hope. I had to believe that.

I still did not know where the bombs had come from, how could I? I had electricity down here, but all I could watch on the TV were my DVDs. There was no newspaper and no radio waves. Hell, I had no idea if there was any kind of civilisation above me.

The folk from the local town, Plainfield, had laughed at me when I was building my bunker, heckled me, called me a freak. Nuclear war had been a possibility, and now the world was being punished for not being ready. For not listening. For not acting.

The construction of my bunker had consumed me in the events leading up to the bombs. I was not married, I had no children, and any friends I had grew tired of playing second fiddle to a seemingly pointless project underground. It probably allowed me to emotionally detach myself from them, and feel little when the possibility that they had all been wiped out became a reality.

I had been a farmer in the old world. I had a farmhand named Billy, who had helped me build my bunker for a bit of extra cash. He had been an enthusiastic, cheerful boy, who had shown an interest in my project. Perhaps he had created one for himself and was out there somewhere. I hoped so.

In the years I had worked with Billy I had grown fond of him. I missed his stories of debauchery on a Monday morning, his endearing clumsiness, and his positive attitude towards life. If he was alive, I hoped that he had retained some of his charm, his ability to uplift a room. The world, somewhere, would need it.

My stocks of tinned food lately had been thinning, and over the last few weeks I had become aware that I would have to finally leave my confinement in search of supplies. I dreamed every day of fresh meat and fruit, but knew the chances of that were minute.

When the bombs had come, I was well prepared. My bunker, though not large, had 4 rooms. The living area had a small single bed, with a TV at the foot of it. A bookshelf sat behind the TV, filled with tales of the old world. I had read them all. Twice.

A small table and chair was on the other side next to a kitchenette, complete with a kettle, a hot plate and a fridge. The fridge did little these days but chill the water that came from a large water tank in the storeroom next door. The storeroom's shelves had once been lined with thousands of cans of all kinds of variations of tinned food - macaroni cheese, chicken and rice, beef stew, ham, tuna, the list was endless. Eating these survival goodies everyday had been merciless on my tastebuds, and they now all tasted the same, bland and boring.

Attached to the storeroom was a toilet. I had built a kind of makeshift plumbing system that resembled a Victorian toilet, a trap door under the toilet sending the excrement down into an air sealed pit down below. I had worried about this not working, but it did, and it had kept the odour at bay. There was no shower, as I would have to use the water sparingly. I cleaned once every couple of days using dry shampoo and body wash, washing it off with a damp cloth,

The final room was home to a small gym. I had a treadmill and a full selection of weights. I felt it was important to stay in shape, who knew what horrors lay above ground. All the electrics had been powered by a generator. In my boredom, I had given the generator a name - Phil, after the darts player, Phil 'The Power' Taylor. Phil's humming noise had been a constant companion in the silence of the underground.

The final item I had in the underground had been my

motorcycle; A Triumph Bonneville T120. It was still in perfect working order, it had been my baby before the bombs. It stared at me every day, dying to be released from it's shackles.

The day had come to finally go above ground. I had cut off my shaggy hair and shaved my beard, in fear that it would interfere with the air seal on my gas mask. My stomach felt tight with fear, with anxiety. What was out there?

As I climbed the ladder to the trapdoor; a large metal disk that resembled a door to a bank vault, memories of the old world, of the farm, of Bill, circled around in my head. I pushed through the trapdoor and held my breath

CHAPTER 2

The New World

A tear formed in my eye.

The misty air hung in the mustardy yellow sky. It was daybreak, but not like a daybreak I had ever seen before. The ground was scarce, devoid of any plants or grass. Bones of the farm animals and birds that had fallen from the sky littered the ground. Insects that had survived the extinction buzzed around my head, the only noise in the silence.

The farmhouse cut a disheveled figure in the background. It looked naked on top of the arid ground. The roof had collapsed, planks of wood circled the dwelling that had crumbled over the years. It bore no resemblance to the building I had called home for almost 40 years.

I walked over to it, and saw the windows had been smashed. Was that from the bombs? The front door was wide open, hanging off its hinges. As I entered what had been the front room, the house provided me with the first answer to my many questions.

The place had been lived in since, that was for sure. A sleeping bag lay on the floor, with an oil lantern on a small table next to it. The new owner was no longer here, the sleeping bag was now covered in dust and debris, becoming at one with its tempered surroundings. What it meant though, was that there were survivors, people were out there.

I decided that I wanted to spend as little time as possible at the farmhouse, the vivid memories of my childhood and adult life at this place had come rushing back.

Now it was nothing but a crippled, looted shell. I looked around for anything that might come in useful, but the place had nothing to offer, the previous occupant had seen to that.

My pulse quickened as I heard a rustling in what used to be the kitchen. Was someone here? I crouched low and loaded the rifle I had bought with me from the bunker. My underground home had been too small for any kind of target practice, so my shooting was as rusty as the appearance of this new world.

I quietly popped my head round, and breathed a sigh of relief as I saw the source of the noise - a boney black cat. It was looking for food, like me, but with no joy. It glared at me, its dark eyes containing many horrors, and quickly made its way over the counter and out of the window. I walked to the opening and watched it peel off across the wasteland, it must have found food recently to be able to move that fast. I took encouragement, and the fact it was even alive.

I left the house and returned to the bunker trapdoor. I had installed a pulley system that had allowed me to get the heavier items down into the bunker. I retrieved the rope from the storeroom and tied it round a shipping crate that I had used as a lift. Placing the motorbike on the lift, I returned to the surface and attached the rope to the pulley system. The bike was heavy, but I managed to successfully tug it to the top. Tying the rope to the base of the pole, I wheeled the bike off the platform, flipping down the kickstand and checking that I had everything I needed for my adventure.

My rucksack contained a couple of extra filters for my mask, 2 tins of canned tomatoes, my last 3 tins of chicken, some ammo for my rifle, a bottle of water, a flick knife and a lighter. I took a sleeping bag with me too. It had occurred to me that if there was people about that they would probably want my bike, and I would be no match for big group, I needed to prepare for the possibility that I may have to return here on foot, and possibly make camp if I got too far away.

In all honesty, I felt a twinge of excitement as I got onto my Triumph and heard the engine roar into life. It had been three years since I had twisted the accelerator and felt the wind pummel my body. The new world awaited.

CHAPTER 3

No Mans Town

As the motorbike screamed across the cracked, dusty roads I felt a freedom and a release that I discovered I had been craving for a long time. The closest town was about a half hour ride away, but that had been with traffic. The roads in the new world were devoid of activity, a runway for myself and my bike.

Looking around I still saw nothing, daybreak had passed but the sky remained full of a heavy fog. I dared not take my mask off, as I did not know if this mist was something more sinister. With little to look at, the land seemed flat and scarce. Aside from the cat, I still had not seen anything that resembled life.

The neighbouring farms were in a similar state to mine, rundown and empty. Their distance from towns and clean water (if there was any) made them poor shelters for anyone left. I didn't see any point in searching them, my farm was further out than these, and it had been looted, so I could not see how these would be any different. I also felt vulnerable out in the open, I fancied my chances better in the concrete jungle that awaited me.

Buildings began to appear around me through the fog, I knew I had made it to the Plainfield. The outskirts were dead, all the doors open and the windows smashed. It had become a familiar sight now, gone were the days of brimming activity - children playing football in the gardens, clothes drying on washing lines in the beating sun. Now it was a cold wilderness, silently weeping in the soft wind.

I decided that I would hide my bike in the outskirts, and

make my way into town on foot. The noise from the engine rose above everything else, and I did not want to attract any unwanted attention. I had a lock with me, and I fastened it to a pipe round the back of one of the broken settlements.

I made my way into the more built up areas, and passed the remains of an old shop. The windows of this were boarded up rather than smashed, but no noise came out of it. I crept round the back and pushed open the rear door. There was no life in here. I checked the main shop, the shelves were empty, and anything that was left was years out of date. I wondered if the boards meant that the shop had been shut before the bombs, or if someone had attempted to make shelter here. I would never find out, and left the shop empty handed.

I was beginning to think that the town was empty, and that bothered me. I needed to get more fuel if I was forced to go further afield, and I had hoped to see other people. I knew this was perhaps very dangerous, what the bombs would have done to people was unimaginable. Everyone would be out for themselves and their family, the scarce resources would no doubt have left people selfish and violent. However, 3 years without the sight or smell of another life had left me craving it, no matter what the cost.

I trudged further into town, to what I remember as the high street. I could faintly make out a noise the far side of the street. I recognised the sound instantly - Phil. It must be a generator, It must be life.

My pulse quickened, and my grip tightened around my rifle. The building it came from loomed ahead through the mist. It had once been a nightclub called Outlaws. Somehow the name had become more fitting in the new world than the old world.

I had been there a few times in my youth, entranced by the strobe lights and intoxicating smell of BO, perfume and jagerbombs. Whilst the scent would have disappeared years ago, I could almost taste it as my brain sent the memories charging around my head.

I knew the building was large inside, their had been 3 floors, and the basement was made up of dark tunnels that had once been full of wide eyed teenagers and loud basey music. It would be a good place to defend, a good place to set up a camp.

I decided I had to go in, I had to see what was left of the world. The front door would be a silly idea. I circled around the building and found a fire escape. I said a little prayer under my breathe, and pulled the handle, it was open.

CHAPTER 4

Outlaws

I slipped quietly inside the club, closing the door silently behind me. It was pitch black, I cursed the fact that I didn't have a torch. I lit my lighter, and could see I was in a narrow corridor. I crept to a doorway, stopping to try and listen for any voices. The sound of the generator was all I could hear. I felt it must have been on this floor, perhaps behind the wall I was keeping close to.

I nudged the door slightly ajar, and peeked through. The next room was lit up with fairy lights all across the ceiling, a couple of the bulbs flickered, but I could see what was in front of me. I was behind the bar. No one was in this room either.

I rummaged around through the bar. There was not much, lots of empty bottles of Vodka, Gin and Tequila. One of the bottles of Tequila still had some in it, and I had an urge to drink it. Knowing I had to keep my wits about me, I stashed it in my bag, it would be a treat if I ever made it out of here.

I made my way around the bar, the floor was covered in empty sleeping bags and empty cans of tinned food. Whoever had lived here had clearly been here a long time. In the far corner was a water tank, but it was empty. That would explain perhaps why whoever was here had left. The sleeping bags reminded me of the one back at the farmhouse, dusty and lifeless.

I knew there was still two more floors to check. Why was the generator still running if no one was here? I decided to check the basement until last, so I crossed the room over the flight of stairs that led to the top floor. Back in the days when the club had been full of activity, the top floor had been a kind of chill out area. People would come up here to chat away from the music, have a drink in peace. Perhaps try and talk their new acquisition into coming home with them.

The double doors at the top of the stairs was shut. I approached them and and gave them a push. Locked.

The lock was on the inside, and the doors looked in fairly good condition, so I decided against trying to break into them. What, or who, were they hiding? If someone was in there, they probably would have heard me pushing the door. I cupped my ear against them, and I thought I could hear the faint sound of a TV. My stomach tightened.

I decided against knocking, and made my way back downstairs. I found the route down to the basement, darkness looming ahead. I held my breath, wondering if this was a good idea. I came here for food, and I highly doubted I would find any down there. My curiosity overpowered me, and I crept down the stairs to the basement to find another set of double doors, these ones were open.

I listened first, I could not hear anything. I was sweating, my heart beating fast. With my rifle at the ready, I eased open the double doors, instantly blinded by the strip lights on the ceiling.

Once my sight returned, in front of me the basement looked a world away from what I remembered. Lit up, it was bigger than I remember. I had only ever been down here under the influence of alcohol and obviously the lights had been off, tripping over passed out revellers who lined the walls.

The lights led me down the tunnel into a wider room. My eyes couldn't believe what I was seeing. The room was clean, the shelves lined with tinned food. A cas RC e of water bottles lay on the floor. Three beds sat side to side in the corner, made up with clean sheets. Nobody was in here, but the place had been used. Life was here.

I lay down on the bed, unsure of how I felt about my discovery. Whoever lived here was well stocked, but where were they? I looked over at the bed side table, and what I saw made my body go numb.

It was a picture in a frame. I knew the couple in the picture, two parents stood behind their son. The boy in the picture was beaming, full of life.

The boy in the picture was Billy.

PART 2

CHAPTER 5

Billy

When the bombs had dropped, Billy had been in bed. Billy liked his bed, enjoyed the soft comfort after a long day working on that dusty old farm. Billy often had company in his bed, he had been a regular at the local nightclub - *Outlaws*. The girls there liked his free spirit, his youthful grin, and he had also managed to develop some muscle working on the farm. Billy was a good looking lad.

On the night of the bombs however, Billy was alone. His parents had been away visiting his grandparents in a village the other side of Plainfield. Billy liked having the house to himself, not having to wash up immediately after his dinner, being able to watch whatever he wanted on the family television. More importantly, he enjoyed being able to partake in his favourite pastime - getting high as a kite - without his parents asking him why his eyes were so red or why he was giggling at a particularly boring news bulletin.

Billy liked working on the farm with his boss, Mr Barton. Billy was probably his only friend. It was hard but rewarding work, but in the months leading up to the bombs, Mr Barton had been more preoccupied with his bunker, which Billy, like everyone else, thought was ridiculous. He had kept his mouth shut and helped where he could though, picking up a few new skills on the way.

Mr Barton had taught him to shoot straight, filter water, stay quiet and even given him a gas mask, which Billy kept at the bottom of his wardrobe, underneath the various clothes that his past conquests had left behind.

When the bombs had fallen, Billy had been stoned, but relatively prepared.

Billy had never built a bunker, like Mr Barton, who was beginning to look like a prophet, had suggested. He had, however, reinforced the family shed, and had filled it with enough items to last a few months. He had done it more so he could take some pictures and earn a few brownie points from Mr Barton, he had no idea that it probably would save his life in the not too distant future.

Life in the shed had been bleak. Sleepless nights with the door being hammered on by raiders, a constant internal battle about if and when he should go and try and find his parents, a hole in the ground for a toilet, no washing, no weed, no girls, no friends.

Eventually the food had run out and Billy knew he had to make the long journey to find supplies and perhaps, if he was lucky, company. He had travelled past Mr Barton's farm, but he knew the man would never let anyone in. Billy was on his own.

It was on his long journey into town that Billy had killed for the first time.

The man had snuck up on him whilst Billy had been resting on the side of the road. Night time had blurred the man's decaying features, but Billy had managed to push him off, grab his own rifle, and shoot the man twice in the chest. It had not killed him instantly, Billy had watched as he coughed and spluttered his way into darkness. Into the silence and mist.

The experience had haunted Billy since, but lately he had grown used to the fact that killing was part and parcel of this new world, this new lawless society.

When Billy had finally made it into what was left of Plainfield, he had spent the first few weeks holed up in an abandoned garage. He had managed to scavenge enough food to eat, but he knew he couldn't stay here, and his journey here had made him terrified to get back on the road home.

One day while he had been out gathering supplies, he had stumbled upon another group of survivors at a pet shop. At first there had been four of them; Thomas, Ellie, Cameron and Donna. The group had taken in Billy, to Cameron's disgust, when they saw he had a gun. The others already owned a pistol, which Thomas had stolen from the corpse of his father, so with the two weapons they had successfully managed to scare away any raiders that had threatened their existence.

Eventually the group decided they needed a new home - the pet shop was cold and small, providing little defence if a bigger group ever came, so they decided upon *Outlaws*. It was the other side of town, where they had not yet been, but the streets were so quiet they thought that Plainfield was more or less abandoned now.

The journey had been easy enough, they did it at night, and managed it without detection. Once they had managed to break into the night club, the place was seemingly untouched, except a locked door on the top floor. Billy could have sworn he could hear a television in there. There were cameras all over the place as well, was someone watching them?

The group had been there for 2 years before Mr Barton had arrived. That side of town had been fruitful for scavenging, and they had even managed to get some beds and an old truck. After about 6 months, Cameron and Ellie, who had become an item, had left to try and find Ellie's son. They never returned.

Billy was no longer the happy, cheerful boy he used to be. He drank all hours of the day, and was always squabbling with Thomas. He had decided his parents were dead, the only memory of them the picture he kept by his bed. There was one thing keeping him sane - he had fallen deeply in love with Donna. She, over time, had grown to love him too, but his drinking had made her keep him at arms length.

CHAPTER 6

A New Group

I woke from my sleep, a little disorientated by the new surroundings, and looked again at the picture of Billy and his family. The idea that he was alive, perhaps living here, had warmed my heart. The room was warm, stocked full of supplies. I decided it would be best to wait here, if Billy was alive, with a group, then my isolation would be over.

A day passed before the footsteps broke the silence. I felt my heart beat faster, my curiosity heightening. The door swung open, and there he was. He looked rough, his hair and beard had grown long and dark. His eyes were bloodshot and the familiar warmth of his face had drained away.

There were two others with him; the man looked a bit older, he was short and stocky, with a shaved head. He carried a pistol on his belt, which was currently pointing at me. His blue eyes piercing into mine. Behind Billy, who I could have sworn was swaying, stood a woman. She had long brown hair with remains of highlights at the tips, tied up in a bun. She was striking, freckles littered her face, the lack of make up showing off her natural beauty, her green eyes also staring into mine, startled at what was in front of her.

"Who the hell are you, how did you get in?!" Shouted the man I did not know, moving closer to me with his pistol held out.

Billy, who had taken a few seconds to process what was going on, stepped forward and put his hand on the pistol, "Put the gun down Thomas, I know this man, used to work for him on that farm I told you about." His words seemed slurred.

"This is the guy with the bunker?" Said Donna, as Thomas lowered his weapon. Billy nodded. "How on earth did you get in, Mr Barton. I thought you had supplies to last you a lifetime old man."

"The door was just open Billy, it's so good to see you! I was sure you were dead, but then I saw the picture, so I stayed, hoped you would return, and here you are," I replied, still stunned to see the boy.

Thomas sloped off and lay down on his bed, angry with Billy for forgetting to lock the door, which seemed like a regular occurrence. Billy pulled out a battered old hip flask and took a drink, his hand visibly shaking.

Billy spent the rest of the day stumbling through the story of how he had wound up here. I felt proud of him, he had listened to a lot of my tips and instructions, but it saddened me to see what the bombs had done to his spirit. It seemed like he had given up, the booze had crippled him.

Over time the other two had warmed to me, they had realised I had valuable skills and was willing to contribute to their day to day lives. It was obvious Billy was infatuated with Donna, and to be honest I was not surprised. She was kind, strong, and gorgeous. It was harder, however, to gauge how she felt about Billy. I thought she liked him, but the drinking obviously was a problem.

Thomas spent most of his time working out, I joined him occasionally, which was probably what impressed him. I went out with him to get food often, and he opened up to me about his childhood. He had been a star football player at college, but never made the cut to the NFL. He had got a job as a bouncer at a nightclub in the city, apparently he had a nickname - 'Tight Thomas,' he could spot a drunk or an underage reveller from miles away, I was curious about how he must feel about Billy's drinking habits, it was a topic that was rarely discussed.

I wondered about the room on the top floor. The others had heard the television too, and sometimes apparently heard noises at night time, but they kept their door locked strictly at night time.

There did not seem much danger in Plainfield, our basement was secure, and there was rarely people about when we went out, but one day that all changed.

CHAPTER 7

Raiders

The gunshot had echoed through *Outlaws,* puncturing through the silence of the morning. We had all been in the basement, we had heard the van arrive outside. It's grizzly engine pulling to a halt seemingly above our heads, followed by the muffled sound of boots landing on the ground above us. The only vehicle noise I had heard in 3 years had been the Triumph and the old van that we had. This noise was louder, more menacing.

We loaded our guns, we had three now, and Donna had become a crack shot as well. A set of footsteps approached the door, why just one set? I felt the adrenaline pump through my body. The figure outside knocked on the door. We did not answer. He began to speak.

"Thomas, Donna, Billy, Mr Barton. My name is Kyle, I'm the man who has been living upstairs. I know you are good people, my cameras have been watching you, to make sure you are not a danger to me. We need to get out of here. There is a big group of raiders searching the area round here, one came in here and I have dealt with him, but someone would have heard the shot. If you want to live, come with me now, they will be able to break in."

Thomas looked at all of us, not moving, it was Donna who got up and opened the door, no one stopped her, all of us just frozen in shock. We had prepared for this moment for months, but none of us were ready.

The man claiming to be called Kyle burst in, his grey hair slicked back and greasy. He wore an old suede overcoat, beneath it a handgun rested on his belt alongside a hunting knife. In his hand he had a shotgun, and on his back a large looking dirty rucksack.

"We need to be quick, they will be back soon, if we work together we can get out of this alive."

We had little other option, so we followed the man, keeping low when we got up to the main bar. On the floor lay the body of the man Kyle had shot, with precision accuracy, in the head. Blood now covered the floor that had once been covered by tequila and beer.

Three more men arrived at the front door, swearing as they saw the body of their fallen comrade. We kept still and quiet, Billy looked in a daze. The three men were all armed, methodically searching around the darkened dance floor. We were behind the bar, and two of the men were approaching from either side.

Billy was entranced, clearly intoxicated. Thomas and Donna both looked alert. Fear, however, was all over their faces. Kyle edged round the corner of the bar, signalling to Thomas to do the same on the other side. Thomas followed his order, and on Kyle's signal, they both fired their weapons.

What followed next we could only tell by the sounds. Two bodies fell to the ground, followed by another gun shot, another body, then a pause, followed finally by another gunshot and the final body to drop to the floor. I had flinched at every shot, four shots, four bodies, three raiders. One of our own had fallen.

We all got up gingerly, Billy struggling now, and then Donna screamed.

Thomas's body lay still on the ground, Kyle standing over him. The bullet had hit him right through his heart. The precision accuracy implied these men must have been trained. His eyes were glassy and still, blood pooling out of him, the floor now a grizzly scene of blood and corpses.

Thomas had died instantly. Donna wept next to him, Billy just stood there, staring blankly. He pulled out his hip flask as a tear rolled down his cheek. My heart went out to them both, Thomas had been a good man, and their only family for over a year, and now he was gone.

Kyle was the first to speak ,"I'm sorry, but we need to get

going, there are more of them out there, they will be coming, you all have a truck right?"

Donna pushed closed Thomas's eyes and stood up, shaking Billy and snatching the flask out of his hand, taking a swig out of it herself before putting it in her pocket. I felt for the boy, but alcohol was not the answer right now.

Kyle led us round to the side door I had used to get in months ago, back in the main room I could hear the shouts of more men arriving, we did not have long.

Kyle pushed the door ajar, and ushered us through. Donna led now, she had come into her own, this girl was made out of steel. It was mistier than ever outside, no doubt the exhaust from their van had added to the haze.

We crept around the back of the building to where our truck was parked, Donna had the keys and jumped into the drivers seat, Billy slid in next to her. Kyle and I leapt into the back.

Donna turned the keys and the truck fired into life, alerting the other raiders. We screeched out of the car park, gunshots now smashing into the side of the truck.

We managed to get out of their eyeline, taking a hard turn off the high street, down into a residential area. We couldn't see far ahead because of the mist, but we managed to negotiate a route that left the raiders far behind us. Their huge truck, while terrifying, would never keep up with us.

"Stop here Donna, let's talk about what we are going to do next" Kyle said, and Donna swung the truck in behind one of the detached houses on the outskirts of town. I had passed this area on my way in, I knew there was nothing here, but we needed to dust ourselves down and take in what had just happened.

We spent most of that night in silence, holed up in one of the abandoned houses. Donna, distraught at the loss of her friend, found solace in the warm embrace of Billy, they both silently drank what they had left, cuddled up solemnly in one corner. Kyle, kept watch most of the night. He was mysterious, but now did not seem to be the time to ask him about himself, so I did my best to get some sleep.

CHAPTER 8

Escaping Plainfield

We survived the night easily enough, the raiders had not followed us. Thomas's passing had hit Billy and Donna hard, they had not really slept, drinking all night. At least they had each other, I thought. I had felt that if they could finally get together, it might help Billy get away from the booze. Strangely, Thomas' death seemed to have bought them closer together, tied at the hip in their grieving.

I had suggested to Kyle that I had a bunker, and now that we had a vehicle, perhaps we could go there for a few days, then return to get supplies from the nightclub once the raiders had passed through. We had locked the door to our basement on the way out, although it was likely they would have broken through.

He seemed to be in agreement. His rucksack had enough food in it to last about a week, so we all clambered back into the truck. There was still little conversation, Donna and Billy now just following whatever we suggested.

Billy had run out of alcohol, and he was shaking, white as a sheet. The withdrawals would be hard, but he needed it. I still had the bottle of tequila that I had found on the day I arrived at *Outlaws,* but I decided I would not tell him about that unless he really needed it.

Kyle was driving this time, with me in the front directing him back to my motorbike. I would then ride that, with them following behind. The truck had plenty of fuel and some more canisters in the back in case.

We arrived back at the bunker later that day, Billy doing a double take - clearly shocked at the difference from the farm he once worked at. He had barely said anything since Thomas had died, and his shakes were getting worse, Donna stayed close to him, deeply concerned. She would fight her own battles another time.

The place was still empty, the farm house looking ugly in the misty back drop. I retrieved the sleeping bag from the house that I had found when I first left the bunker, and told Donna and Billy that they could have the bed if they wished. Donna looked awkward, but nodded, they had basically spent the night in each others arms last night, what difference would it make. She wanted to be close to Billy, found comfort in him, and Billy needed looking after.

Kyle said he would sleep in the truck on the first night, keep watch in case we had been followed. I was certain if we had been followed we would have heard them, but nonetheless I agreed. I slept on the floor in the dusty sleeping bag

The next morning, Kyle, clearly impressed with my set up in the bunker, heated up some of the tinned soup, and we ate, still in silence. Donna and Billy were still inseparable. Billy looked a bit better this morning, but was still hardly talking.

That night, Donna had said that she and Billy would keep watch together. She knew Kyle needed some sleep. I wanted to do it, but I knew she would not be talked out of it. As they scurried up the ladder, I wanted to talk to Kyle, find out more about this mysterious man who had spent so long watching us. Then saving us.

However, once I had used the toilet, I returned to see him snoring in the bed, peacefully sleeping. It looked like I would be on the floor again, I would leave the questioning for another day.

We both woke up to a rumbling noise above us. It was a noise we had heard before, only days ago. It was the van, how had they followed us? Kyle leapt up, grabbing his shotgun and rushing up the ladder, I followed, my heart once again pumping.

We just about caught sight of the huge van disappearing into the mist. My heart sank as I looked over at the truck, it was empty. Donna and Billy were gone.

I opened the door to check for any blood, there was none, and their blanket was on the back seat, they must have fallen asleep. My bottle of Tequila was on the floor, I picked it up and cursed, it was empty. They had stolen it, drank it, and passed out. Now I see why they wanted to keep watch

Before giving up hope, I caught site of a note attached to the windscreen wipers.

They are alive, give us the old man, we will give them back unharmed. We are in the city, at the courthouse, he will know where that is.
Don't trust him.

PART 3

CHAPTER 9

Kyle

I felt completely numb, who was this man standing at the end of the barrel of my gun. Why was he so calm in the face of his death. He had cost me the one person left in this world who I cared about.

My hand shook as I demanded answers from Kyle, why did the raiders want him, what was it that he had done that meant his reward would be the lives of two innocent humans.

"If you take that thing out of my face, old man, I will tell you everything, I can fix this but I need your help." Kyle said, still looking strangely calm.

I did not trust him, the note told me explicitly not to trust him, but Billy and Donna's lives were on the line, I did not feel like I had much of a choice.

We went back down into the bunker. My sweaty hands still holding the note and my gun. Kyle sat down, lighting a cigarette. Strange, I couldn't remember him smoking before, and began to tell his story.

Kyle did not say much about his life before the bombs dropped, I guess he did not need to. He mentioned that he was ex army, hence the jacket and his combat ability, and that he had retired to live in the countryside with his wife - Judy.

He had a keen interest in science, and used to run experiments at their home - in the vast countryside on the other side of the city. It was his love of science that had meant he had been relatively prepared for the bombs - he owned plenty of gas masks, and knew how to do basic things such as filtering water.

The bombs had missed their home, but there was a big problem - Judy had type 1 diabetes, and it did not take long for the both of them to run out of Insulin.

It was his love for Judy and his determination to keep her alive that landed him totally isolated at the nightclub.

He had ventured into the city in the hope of finding some insulin when he stumbled across the group, then in it's infancy, that had ended up taking Billy and Donna.

He had been searching through an old pharmacy when he had been taken by one of the group's henchman, and it was his ability to overpower the man easily and disarm him that caught the attention of the groups leader, a huge, muscley, terrifying man named Drago.

Kyle was almost certain that Drago had been in prison before the bombs, given his lack of a moral compass. Kyle did appreciate, however, that this new world was doing terrible things to people.

Drago had decided to take Kyle in, thinking that he would be useful in his group. Kyle, once he heard about the extensive amounts of medical supplies they had gathered, agreed, quickly formulating a plan to steal what he needed - he knew he would not have long before Judy ran out of insulin back at home.

Drago had a son, an equally nasty piece of work, called Cole, who also struggled with diabetes. I knew where this was going. Kyle decided when he saw Cole kill an innocent family simply for their meagre supplies of food that Judy was far more deserving of life than Cole.

When Kyle managed to steal what Insulin Drago had, he escaped, managing to get back to his home, his wife Judy still alive. He could not however sleep anymore with his eyes shut, crippled with anxiety.

Kyle and Judy lived in fear for almost a year at their home, but it was on one of his scavenging hunts in the local area that Kyle was captured, again, by one of Drago's henchmen.

This man laughed as he told Kyle that Drago's son was gravely ill and Kyle was the most wanted man in the New World. Kyle managed to escape this mans grip, and kill him, but knew that Drago was closing in, so went home to get Judy, where he decided to take them to Plainfield - far enough from Drago's city, but also embedded in a concrete jungle.

They made it to the nightclub, and scavenged enough food in the first few weeks that would last them years - which is when he barricaded them into the top floor of *Outlaws*.

This was where Kyle and Judy remained - the nightclub generator still worked, and the CCTV system was operational, but he was riddled with fear, and naturally terrified when Billy and his group moved in downstairs.

Kyle soon realised the group were harmless to him - they also just wanted survival, but he was too afraid to ever meet them, so he remained upstairs, occasionally coming out at night when the others were asleep to get some food, or grab some booze from the fully stocked bar.

Judy's condition deteriorated around four months ago, and Kyle could not understand why. They still had insulin, but without a doctor or the right equipment, he was never able to find out why. Eventually, she passed away, and Kyle's devastation was almost too much to bare.

He decided that he would have to go out and bury her body, it could not stay with him in his stronghold. One night, when the group had drank themselves to sleep, he ventured out with her body - he wept as he buried her just outside the city.

What he did not know at the time, however, is that he was seen.

Once he arrived back, he drank and he drank, his sorrow overwhelming his body, he had now lost everything, he decided that his life was not worth living, but it was as he was preparing his rifle to put in his mouth that he heard the truck - recognising it instantly as Drago's, the men he saw on the CCTV confirming that.

He knew that the others did not deserve to die because of his mistakes - and he also knew that Drago would not hesitate to kill the others for their supplies. He had found a purpose, prepared himself, and headed downstairs, introducing himself for the first time to the occupants downstairs.

CHAPTER 10

Back to Outlaws

Kyle stubbed out his fourth cigarette, he had been chain smoking since he started telling his story - his hands were shaking, and tears forming in his eyes. I had lowered my rifle, the emotional power of his story had left me in no doubt that what he was saying was true.

As much as I felt sorry for the man, Billy and Donna were still in grave danger and we needed to address that. I did not have time to sympathise with this troubled man just yet.

Kyle, stood up, appearing to dust himself off, looking driven now, satisfied that I believed him.

"I have got a plan, but it is going to be dangerous. We got to get back to the nightclub, where all the Insulin is, they will not have been able to get it - they may have got into my floor, but they will not have found the safe, and if by chance they have, there is no way they will know the code."

"If we can get the Insulin that I have left, then I can take them to Drago. I will have to give myself to him as well, but I have nothing left to live for. If we do that, then he may let your friends go. We have time, he will not kill them otherwise he loses his bargaining chip - and his son will die. I suggest we rest a couple of days, and hopefully by then the nightclub will be deserted."

I pondered the plan, and decided he was probably right -this seemed to be the best course of action. I wondered why they did not just wait outside the bunker for us to come out, but they knew Kyle, they knew he was smart - far better to have something that he needed. Something that would stop him from just keeping quiet or killing himself. Drago needed him alive, and needed him to have reason to talk.

We spent the next few days in the bunker - we ate the rest of the food that Kyle had, but hardly talked. He was a quiet man, that was for sure. To be honest, I did not want to speak much either - life before I left the bunker had been easier, perhaps I preferred it all along on my own.

After three days of silence, it was now time to enter the mist.

As we left the bunker, I half expected there to be a welcoming party on top, but there were no men there, they wanted the Insulin. They would wait for us to come to them.

We took separate vehicles back to Plainfield, I had my bike, now with plenty of fuel, roaring down the dusty road ahead of Kyle in the truck. I felt tense, my blood was pumping quickly as we travelled back to town, the anticipation of what was to come circling my thoughts. Kyles story still troubled me, the old man had been through a hell of a lot, and it was by no means even close to being over.

We arrived into Plainfield at night, the mist laying particularly low on this particular one. The buidlings, silently telling a thousand stories, watched us as we hid our vehicles, taking the last stretch to the nightclub on foot, in case they were waiting for us.

We shuffled round to the back of the nightclub, the torch illuminating the back door, it was open.

Kyle signalled that he would go first, and crept in. The place seemed deserted.

Inside the main room, the dead bodies of the men had been taken away, but Thomas still lay there, the scent was unbearable. The sight of a dead body sent shivers all the way through my body, I would never get used to that. Kyle found a sheet and threw it over him before taking him outside, muttering words that I could not understand. I watched as he placed the body down outside, then threw up, the smell throwing his stomach from side to side.

Back in the club, Kyle led the way up to his floor - quickly we saw that the doors had been smashed open.

The remnants of Kyle's fortress were all over the floor. The TV we had heard on countless times had been smashed, the sofa ripped open, fluff and fabric littering the place. I watched as Kyle quietly walked over to the photo of his wife that lay on the floor, and slid the photo out of the cracked glass, pausing for a second as he stared at it. He then quietly slipped it into his bag.

I wished, in that moment, that I had some memento of my family, of my loved ones, I had nothing.

"Safe is this way, if they didn't take the whole damn thing with them. Savages," said Kyle, I thought I could see a tear in his eye.

We went through the wreckage, into what must have been his toilet. It had been smashed apart, like the rest of his house. He had picked up a crowbar, and jammed it behind the shower tray.

It came up easily, clearly he had done this many times. Underneath the shower tray he removed the loose floorboards - and underneath them, he put his hands in and pulled out a small safe. It reminded me of the old mini bars you had in hotel rooms, before the bombs. The brief memory of my old life sent a shiver down my spine.

The safe was code-locked, and it made a small squeak as he tapped in the digits. It clicked as he opened it, and pulled out a carrier bag full of medicine.

Kyle turned to me, and I thought I saw him smile for the first time.

"Ready to go and see Drago?"

CHAPTER 11

Captured

Billy had spotted the Tequila in Mr Barton's dirty old bag when they had arrived at the bunker, and once he had seen it, he could not get it out of his mind. He was riddled with grief for Thomas, Donna's warm embrace the only comfort in this trying time.

The night they had spent in the bed together he had not slept, and neither had Donna. They did not speak either, merely held each other. The next morning, even though Billy felt he was getting over his withdrawals, he wanted the Tequila to take him away from this horrible place. When he told Donna about it, she looked at him blankly, and simply nodded. It was her who took the Tequila, and said that they would take the evening watch.

Billy and Donna sat in the back of the truck, sipping the bottle, both locked in thought about their friend. For Billy, the Tequila allowed him to finally speak, even if only a little, and made him feel stronger. Donna quietly cried, but the alcohol eased her pain. Later on that evening, Billy and Donna kissed for the first time, and shortly after they made love.

Momentarily, Billy was taken away from the troubles of this world, he had always loved Donna, and he would never forget this night. For Donna, she had succumbed to her feelings for the damaged man she tried so hard not to love.

Afterwards, they slowly fell asleep in each others arms, still silent, and the mist descended upon them.

The Tequila had finally allowed them to temporarily escape

their pain, and find solace in each other, however artificially it may have been.

When Drago's men arrived, they found the two of them fast asleep, it was the easiest kidnapping they would ever make. The first thing Billy saw when he awoke was not Donna. It was a sweaty, scarred man - who smiled at him shortly before knocking him back out again with the butt of his weapon.

When Donna came to, her head was pounding - she was not much of a drinker, and her body was not agreeing with what it had been through. She froze as she heard the rumbling of an engine, then looked around and saw that Billy's arms were no longer wrapped around her - she was in a van.

She slowly got her bearings, terrified to see Billy tied up beside her, they were in the back. They had been taken. She cursed the Tequila, all the memories of last night flooding back into her conscious mind. She felt helpless, Billy was still out of it. Still. Motionless.

She felt sick with anxiety, her hangover escalating her feelings. She had felt so safe with Billy last night, she did not regret that. But it was her idea to drink the Tequila, and she felt her stupidity had lead to this horrible situation.

The journey to wherever they were going seemed never-ending. The back of the van had no windows, it was empty and dark. Her mouth was so dry, and she felt the tears roll down her cheeks again.

The van finally came to a halt and there was silence. Billy was awake now, but his mouth was taped, and he simply sat there, staring at her.

The back door flew open, and the light came rushing in, stinging her vulnerable eyes. A group of silhouettes appeared, eventually taking the shape of the dirty, sinister men that had captured them.

She was thrown to her feet, the men around her laughing, slapping and touching her. She hated it. They were being shown into a huge building, decrepit and lifeless. She recognised the front from old newspapers - it was the courthouse in the city. It was well defended, a metal fence snaked around the outside, topped with sharp and menacing barbed wire. More men wandered around the gate, all armed with weapons ranging from shotguns to baseball bats. They were all dirty, malnourished, their clothes ripped and bloody. Yet they all smiled a sinister smile at her, their eyes filled with the evils of the new world.

They were taken into the courthouse, Billy was still in a daze. He no longer cared about his safety, but he would make them pay for anything they did to Donna. Last night had been euphoric, an outpouring of physical feelings, and now any happiness he had found had instantly been snatched away.

Inside the courthouse was a miserable place. Dirty sleeping bags lined the floor, mouldy food and dirt everywhere. They went past a group playing cards on top of a broken fridge, and Billy could smell the alcohol in their glasses, he needed a drink. He watched Donna, she was expressionless, but she looked strong. She was always strong.

Eventually they reached the outside of a door, reinforced with wooden planks nailed across the glass window it once had. The door was opened with a key, and they were thrown in. One man came in with them, the man who had knocked Billy out. He dropped a bottle of water at Billy's feet, and removed the tape on their mouths, and the rope on their wrists.

"Boss says he needs you two alive, you try anything, we kill you and your friends. He will be in to see you soon." The man said, before sneering at them and leaving, clicking the door shut behind them.

Their cell was once an old office, it was now looted and empty, the windows also covered with wooden planks. They had gone up a few flights of stairs on their way up - so they knew getting out of the window, even if they had the strength to prise of the wooden planks, was not an option.

Billy fell against the wall, and slid down, sitting with his head in his hands. Donna immediately went to him, and they embraced again, still without saying anything. Words were not needed, they just needed comfort from each other.

Later that night, at least they thought it was night, a huge man unlocked the door and came in. He eyed them both, and smiled, baring his rotten yellow teeth. He wore a vest, his tattooed, muscly arms crossed at his chest. His hair shaved, a scar running down the side of his head.

"You two made the wrong friend. That man you were with, he took something very important to me, we need him - and therefore we need you two to get him back. An eye for an eye, they say. Try anything I will make you watch as I cause the other unimaginable pain. Don't think i'm messing around. Now get some rest, I don't need you two dying on me."

He left, chuckling to himself. Later on one of his henchmen came in with half a sandwich each. Donna and Billy wondered what Kyle had done, angry at him now. They ate, and sat once again in silence, comforting each other, and waiting.

CHAPTER 12

The City

As we left the nightclub for the last time, I headed downstairs and grabbed Billy's picture of his family. The rest of our hideout had been looted, the beds torn apart, and any food or water had been taken.

We headed back to our vehicles, we had decided again to take both, if we needed to escape we would have a better chance with both the truck and the motorbike. Plus, I had no intention of deserting my beloved Triumph.

We left again at night time - the city was about a two hour drive from Plainfield, but it stretched over a vast area, and there would no doubt be other threats aside from Drago's group. Kyle had said their numbers were great when he lived amongst them, and now they would probably be even larger and more terrifying.

This night, like all others, was misty and dark, the silence around us penetrated by the growl of our engines. The highway to the city was littered with deserted cars, and the fog that surrounded the road occasionally infiltrated by campfires and lights from survivors in the distance.

I knew that we must have been getting close to the city when the tyres on Kyle's truck, suddenly exploded.

I watched as the car veered of and smashed into one of the deserted vehicles, coming to rest with it's bonnet crumpled and steamy.

I screeched to a halt, my heart thumping again. I needed Kyle.

I dismounted the bike, and wandered around to the passenger

side of the truck. Kyle's head was slumped against the steering wheel, crimson blood leaking out of a gash on his forehead. He was still breathing.

I ripped off a bit of my shirt and pressed it to his forehead, gently shaking him, when I heard the movement behind me.

"Well hello there, sorry about your friend, now step away from the car," said the croaky, feminine voice behind me.

I dropped the rag and turned around slowly. It was a woman, her dirty greasy hair hanging around her haggard face. She was holding a knife. She was incredibly thin, and wore filthy clothes three sizes too big.

"Heres how this is going to go down, I am going to take your bike, and your clothes, and your weapons, and you are not going to resist, or I will cut your throat," she said, as her dark eyes stared into mine.

She moved closer to me, when suddenly a gunshot rang out behind me, and her face exploded.

Her body slumped to the floor, some of the blood spatter landing on my clothes. I turned and saw Kyle hanging limply out the window.

The rifle dropped to the dirty tarmac with a clatter, and Kyle fell forward, the last of his energy used up to save my life, and give Billy and Donna a chance.

Dazed, I tried to shake him, I feared the worst. I put my fingers to his bloody neck, but I felt nothing. My brain went blank briefly, trying to process what had just happened.

Kyle was dead.

I was now on my own, and suddenly the task ahead seemed almost impossible. Kyle knew these people, he had a plan - and also they wanted him alive, would his death make any difference as long as they got the insulin.

I smashed my fist against the truck, and cursed to the heavens, I had never felt so alone. I spat at the corpse of the dead woman, the wanderer who had cost me everything, and Kyle his life.

I sat for a while, in a state of confusion and grief. I hoped Kyle was with his wife now, and that he would be watching over me. I would never forget what the man did for me, even if it is his fault that Billy and Donna are captive. I thought about them for a bit, happy that they at least had each other.

When i was ready, I grabbed what equipment Kyle had - his gun, his coat, his knife, the insulin, and then found his cigarettes. I did not smoke, but now seemed a good time to start - the nicotine rush made me feel light and woozy for a second, taking me away from the horrific situation ahead of me.

I trudged down the road, and found the spikes that had destroyed Kyle's tyres. I cursed, such a simple way to end someone's life.

I got my things together and pulled Kyles limp body out of the truck, putting him to the side of the road and covering him with a sheet I found in a nearby vehicle. I did not have a shovel, I felt guilty not burying him - but he would have wanted me to press on.

I carefully wheeled the Triumph around the spikes, and said goodbye to the old man. The engine roared back into life, and it was not long before I was deep in the concrete labyrinth of the city.

I knew my way around - and I found a suitable place to stash my motorbike, walking a couple of hundred yards before I turned a corner, taking a breath as the courthouse loomed ahead of me through the fog. A fence had been built around it, that would be my first challenge.

The streets were a mess, moss growing through cracks in the road, smashed windows and boarded up shops all around me. The soul of the place had been taken and replaced with an underlying evil. There was nothing but silence and mist.

I loaded my rifle, and headed towards the courthouse.

CHAPTER 13

Inside the Courthouse

Without Kyle, and his calming presence, I was unsure of what to do. Did I walk in and hand over the Insulin, hoping the news of the old man's passing and the medicine would be enough to convince Drago (who did not sound like a particularly reasonable man), to hand over Billy and Donna.

I decided that first I would try and get an idea of what I was up against, scope the place out. I made my way around the rusty fence, the silence of the night now penetrated with voices and drunken laughter on the other side.

The building itself, one of the largest in the city - was shrouded in darkness. Only a handful of the windows of the large, square shaped, crumbling antique were illuminated with light. Most of the windows had been boarded up, and none of them had any glass In them anymore.

At the rear of the fence, where the murmurs had quietened, I made my move. A car lay deserted at the base of the fence, and I stepped up onto it. I took off the thick jacket I had taken off Kyle, and placed it over the top of the barbed wire. I said a short prayer, then shifted my weight up and over the fence., landing with a muffled thud that did not attract any unwanted attention.

The alleyway in front of me was dark, and I knew it led round the front of the courthouse. The floor was littered with food tins, beer bottles and cigarette butts - and I had little doubt there would be a patrol. However it seemed all Drago's men did throughout the night was drink - they probably rarely had people breaking in, the fear they oozed enough to keep people out on its own.

I needed a way into the building. I slowly made my way to the end of the grubby alleyway, careful not to knock into any of the beer bottles. I pocked my head around the corner, and what I saw gave me hope. There were only a handful of men, two were sat around a three legged table, the other side of what looked like an entrance into the building. They looked long passed out, the empty spirit bottles on the table confirming my suspicions. The main gate was further down, and the guards outside that were also sat down. They looked awake, I would need to try the door closest to me, and slide in silently, otherwise the guards at the gate would see me

I crept round to the doorway, and the men did not stir. With my rifle raised, in case of any movement, I leant on the door, and it pushed open. Silently, I slid into the room. I could feel the adrenaline, in some ways I enjoyed it, the life I had been living before I left the bunker was so safe, so consistent, and so boring.

The room I came into turned out to be the far corner of a large foyer, with the main entrance further down. The floor was littered with sleeping bags, men and their weapons scattered around, with various grunting snores emanating from their alcohol fuelled sleeps. The place stank of stale beer and body odour, and it was a mess. These men were nothing more than foot soldiers, put to work like dogs in exchange for a roof over their heads, companions, and a steady stream of booze. The world had become a dark place.

The only option from here was to go up the stairs. I knew Billy and Donna were likely in a room that was locked and I would need a key. I had no idea what he looked like, or where he was likely to be.

Light flickered up the grand staircase that looped around the sleeping bodies on the floor, and I had a clear route up to the first step. I slowly made my way through the bodies, my heart jumping every time one of the men stirred, and then rose up the staircase, keeping the creaks to a minimum.

The stairs led to a long corridor, with men nowhere to be seen. I started creeping down the corridor, and stopped dead when I heard low voices coming out of an open doorway. I pressed my back against the wall, the conversation was about little more than women and cards. I hoped these voices might spill some valuable information, but I was to be disappointed.

I started heading the other way, down to the end of the corridor and taking a right. At the end of what was in front of me was another staircase, and more darkness. I shuffled forward, stopping before every doorway. I was deep in their fortress now.

As I got near the next staircase, one of the doors was open, but no voices came out of it. I looked in.

My heart stopped as I locked eyes with a boy sitting up in the bed, he was white as a sheet, dark red around the eyes, and his skin hung from his bones. He looked just as scared as I was, I lifted my rifle up, pointing it at his head, even though I knew this person was not a threat. I could not afford for him to alert anyone else.

The boy coughed and lay back down on the bed, I could practically hear his bones creaking.

"who are you....my daddy will kill you... get out of here," the boy spluttered.

The realisation hit me quick, this was Cole. Drago's son. He looked awful, it was hard to believe that this boy in front of me was capable of killing. I had what he needed, however, and I could use that to my advantage.

I knew what I had to do.

CHAPTER 14

Silence and Mist

Billy and Donna thought it had been about five days since they had been locked away in their cell. For Billy, the first few days had been horrendous, the withdrawals taking over his body. He was sweaty yet shivery, often felt nauseous, and struggled to sleep.

By what they thought was the fourth day, he had begun to feel better. Donna had looked after him, talked to him through the day, held him at night. Their bond had become unbreakable. He did not feel he would have survived if she had not been there. Her strength had empowered him.

Words had begun to creep back into his mouth, and they had spent the last night in their cell talking - remembering Thomas, talking about their future together, ignoring their captive status. It warmed them both. Billy told Donna that he loved her, that he had always loved her. She looked deep into his eyes, and gently kissed his dry, cracked lips, and said it back to him. He slept better that night than he had done in years.

Their sleep was interrupted however, when the door was flung open, in what felt the early hours of the morning. It was Drago - and he looked angry, his face red, his eyes slits. Sweat fell from his brow.

"Get up, and follow me," he had ordered.

He had not tied them up, or even put tape on their mouths. He led them out of their cell, both their legs wobbly at first, struggling to hold up their body weight.

Drago led them through the courthouse, he travelled quickly, an unusual anxiety leaking out of his movements.

They arrived at the foyer - all the soldiers were awake now. Their sinister faces now pale and nervous. What was going on?

They passed through the large entrance doors at the front of the foyer, the tension was thick in the air. Nobody spoke.

Out in the yard, Billy and Donna immediately heard the familiar rumble of the truck engine, the truck that had bought them to this forsaken place.

Billy's mouth dropped open when he caught sight of the vehicle, and the man stood in front of it - a gun held to the head of a rather ill looking boy.

"Billy, Donna, get in the van now. Drago, you try anything, and I put a bullet through your boy's head."

Drago looked over at Billy and Donna, and nodded to them. The pair of them slowly moved away, and past Mr Barton and Cole. They slid into the front of the van. Mr Barton noticed that they were grasping each others hands, and he allowed himself a little smile.

"Billy, you ok to drive?" Mr Barton shouted. Billy nodded, releasing Donna's hand as he edged over to the drivers seat.

Mr Barton moved round to the passenger door, still holding Cole. With one hand, he took the bag of Insulin out of his backpack, and threw it to Drago's feet. When Drago knelt down to get it, Mr Barton pushed Cole forward, the boy falling, and leapt into the other passenger seat. Billy, knowing what he had to do, cranked the truck into gear, and pressed his foot firmly on the gas - the truck exploding forwards and through the gate.

Shots rattled out around the truck, but it was huge. One of the bullets exploded through the wing mirror.

Billy looked at the dashboard, a red light blinking at him.

"Theres no fuel!" he shouted.

Behind them, two smaller motorbikes came flying out of the gate, in hot pursuit of them. Mr Barton leant out the window, firing shots back at them.

One of his shots connected, and the man on the motorcycle flew backwards, as if his body had hit an invisible wall. Mr Barton shouted with joy, but that was quickly countered with a curse as he realised it was the last of his bullets.

The lone motorcyclist chased them through the city, but eventually the truck coughed and spluttered and grinded to a halt.

The three of them sat in silence, defeated. They had no weapons, no way out of this now. Drago would surely kill them.

Donna watched in the wing mirror that was still useable as the man on the motorcycle approached them slowly, his rifle raised, a black helmet sat on his head.

As the man got to the window, Billy and Donna were holding hands again, resigning themselves to death, at least they would die together. Mr Barton sat in silence, he had been so close.

The three of them watched, and their jaw dropped for the last time that day, as the man lowered his rifle and took off his helmet.

It was Cameron.

The man who had left over a year ago with his partner, Ellie, to find her son. They thought he was dead - yet here he was.

"Alright Bil, Donna! Not sure I know this one, good shot though. Got room for me in there? I need to get away from these people. They are savages. They murdered Ellie. We need to get as far away from here as possible."

All three of them stared at him, completely stunned. Mr Barton opened the door, and Cameron got in. Donna, after a few moments, put her arms around him and squeezed him.

"Thank you Cameron, thank you. I'm so sorry about Ellie. Thank God you're OK"

Tears were in her eyes, and they slowly crept into his. The relief of getting away from those people was all over his face, but the horrors of his time in their company had no doubt affected him, it was unlikely he had even had a chance to grieve for Ellie. He was free now, just like the rest of them. But his scars would haunt him forever.

Mr Barton broke the silence to say that his bike was nearby - and if they doubled up on the two bikes, then they would be able to get away. Cameron took Mr Barton to retrieve his bike, and when they returned, the four of them sped off together, their hearts now full of hope - into the silence and mist.

EPILOGUE

Billy and I stood side by side, admiring our handy work. I looked at him, and he grinned at me, that cheeky grin that I had long forgotten.

We gazed at our new home - We had travelled far away from the city, and found a farm that seemed in fairly good shape. Well, it still had a roof. Between us, we rebuilt it, and made it strong, weatherproof, and cosy. Most importantly, Billy and Donna had their own room - young love could be noisy at times. On the mantlepiece stood two pictures - one of Ellie, which Cameron had kept with him, and the one of Billy and his parents. He still harboured hopes of them being alive.

When we had settled in, we had held a proper funeral for Thomas, Ellie and Kyle. Cameron had been allowed to grieve - and then we had been able to move forward.

Donna came out, and put her arms around Billy, and we watched as Cameron's motorcycle roared towards us - he had been out gathering supplies, and his bag today looked particularly full. I hoped he had some tinned chicken. That was my favourite these days.

In the months since we escaped the city, the mist had started to lift, the sun once again beginning to shine through. The days had become lighter, and colour had returned to our skins.

Billy and I had been digging through the cracked, arid land, the sun had softened it enough that we thought it might be possible to start growing some fruit or some vegetables in the soil we found underneath. Cameron had located some seeds on one of his trips.

We all looked at the ground, a small plant beginning to show through the soil. Donna broke the silence.

"Come on farmers, let's get inside, looks like dinner has arrived."

The three of them went inside, but I stayed for a second, surveying the hope that surrounded me. I had been wrong all these years, people were not so bad.

Girl Allergies

"First love is only a little foolishness and a lot of curiosity"

- George Bernard Shaw

PART 1

PIPER

She was beautiful, and the big problem was, I knew it. The issue was never asking girls out, it was actually going out with them. On this occasion it was Piper. She was warm, kind and attractive. An added bonus was she knew barely anything about me. However, it became apparent that the same problems were emerging like wildfire.

Last Thursday, our Chemistry teacher, Mr Cripps, had relayed to me the most exciting bit of information I had heard from him all year; the empty desk to my right was to be taken up by a new girl.

The other students, bizarrely, given it was only half way through the Christmas term, were already apparently bonded by blood, and therefore seemingly uninterested in a new student. Don't get me wrong, I had close friends, I could even count them on two hands, but what I really wanted was a girlfriend, my first girlfriend, or at the very least, a girl that I could take to the Christmas dance.

At first glance, I was not particularly unattractive. I held down a place in the school football team, sported a fairly basic but popular chestnut brown haircut, and liked to think I had a fairly sharp turn of wit. Girls, in general, tended to say yes if I asked them to go for the customary walk. A walk was essentially a first date, given that at school you could not exactly whisk another student off to a restaurant or a bar. If it went well, then the world of Friday nights at the local Bowling Alley, might just become a reality.

The problem was my skin. It was like I was allergic to a woman that was interested in me.

It would usually go like this - about 5 minutes into the walk, once we had escaped view of the school, my skin would start to feel warm. The warmth would become unbearable to the point that I simply had to scratch it. I had eczema as a child, and the sensation was no different. Soon after, the itching would become uncontrollable, like I had ants crawling all over my body. I would not be able to concentrate on the confused girl by my side, and usually they would find a way to retreat back to school.

It was embarrassing, and at this point most of the girls at school had heard about my complication. Nicknames had emerged, and my confidence was beginning to wane. I knew that girls were aware of it, so now I'd be lucky to make it 2 minutes into the walk without the twitching and scratching taking hold of me.

Piper however, would have no idea of my troubles. She had long blonde her and minty green eyes. Previously, she had lived in Newcastle, and her northern accent immediately made her stand out from her west country peers.

Mr Cripps, quickly becoming my favourite teacher, paired us up for our Chemistry assignment on her first morning. It became apparent that Piper had no interest in Chemistry, allowing me to get to know her a bit better. It all seemed to be going well, she laughed at my humour, asked me about myself, and I think I even caught her staring at me. Why could I talk to girls in the 'safety' of our Chemistry Lab but not outside of school?

Eventually, I plucked up the courage to ask her on the dreaded walk. Unsure of whether she knew what that meant, she agreed with a smile. She also asked for my number, and text me that night saying that she was looking forward to our walk tomorrow. Clearly, she knew. Damn.

PART 2

BAILEY

Piper and I set off, and immediately I could feel the itching coming. She was busy talking about her Northern heritage, how her Dad had never got over the mining strike and thats why they had finally shut up shop and moved down South, how her older brother hated the idea of living with us 'scrawny southerners.'

I couldn't concentrate. I couldn't participate. I couldn't impress her.

"You alright pet," she asked. My heart sank. Then it came. It felt like a burning hot poker had been pressed between my shoulder blades, and I started scratching like I had never scratched before.

Needless, to say, the walk didn't last much longer. Piper became another hopeless venture, and, aside from our Chemistry project, conversation between us ceased to exist. The boys laughed and the girls giggled, all except my best friend Bailey, who was exceptionally-uncool-and-therefore-cooler-than-everyone-else.

I had been friends with Bailey since I was about 10, and therefore had never seen her as a love interest. However, we were always able to spend time together just the two of us. My problems with girls had started about the same time I had hit puberty, therefore I was already totally comfortable around Bailey.

Naturally, she found my problems with women hilarious, but was always a shoulder to cry on. I did, however, feel like asking her to the dance would be slightly giving up hope. Settling if you will.

Bailey was very confident. That much was for sure. She was

quite short, with long black hair and dark, unreadable eyes. She always wore t shirts blazoned with her favourite bands. She wasn't a goth, more of a rock chick, I suppose. She knew how to make me feel better, and baked one of the best cookie and cream cheesecakes you will ever eat.

One night, we were eating her cheesecake and doing our usual thing - listening to her latest vinyl and playing Mario Kart, she asked me if I actually knew how to dance.

It struck me that I didn't. I had been trying to get these women to go to a dance with me - but not only did I have this skin condition, but I did not actually know how to dance! In all honest she did not seem like the kind of girl that would be into the typical school slow dance, but she said she had lessons when she was younger.

She offered to teach me, and put forward the argument that it might help me be a bit closer to girls. I doubted it, given that Bailey and I had shared a bed uncountable times when we had sleepovers.

Bailey selected *Thinking of you,* by Ed Sheeran, and came close. I put my arms around her hip, as she put hers around my neck. Clumsily, we shuffled around the room. I stood on her toe and she laughed. Wait a minute, her laugh, it was different, it sounded cute, almost flirtatious. My grip tightened as she softly said into my ear that I was doing well. What was happening.

The music stopped, but she did not let go, and neither did I. She leant back, still with her arms around my neck, and stared into my eyes. Her dark eyes. I felt this energy, almost an intoxication. Was Bailey the answer. Did I fancy Bailey?

She stepped back, and gave me a cheeky grin.

''Would you like to go to the dance with me," I blurted out. She nodded, not with her usual confidence, but with a shyness I had never seen from her. Had she just experienced the same thing as me?

"Your going to need some more lessons though." I laughed at this, and immediately felt comfortable again, as she took her Doc Martins off to examine her toe.

Soon after my mum arrived to take me home. Bailey gave me a hug goodbye, but this time with a kiss on the cheek. She never gave me a kiss on the cheek.

At no point did I need to scratch. At no point did I sweat. But there was one overwhelming feeling. I liked Bailey. My best friend.

PART 3

THE DANCE

I could not stop thinking about Bailey. I had not seen her since that night, exams at the end of term had meant that it was impossible. We had texted, but I felt that the dynamic had changed. We no longer talked about my girl struggles, my scratching, the kids at school. Now we talked about each other, as if we had only just met for the first time, as if we were preparing for a first date.

I had fears. When Bailey had given me the dancing lesson the feelings had come from nowhere. I had no time to think about the scratching. I was completely caught up in the moment. It was definitely a moment. The time since then had made me realise I definitely did like her, therefore I had become anxious, and my scratching had flared up even with Bailey not there. She knew about it, and I was certain she would not treat it like the other girls. As the dance approached, I was certain I would not get away without it happening.

The day of the dance had come round. I was to meet Bailey at her house and my mum was going to give us a lift over to the school. I Had spent almost 2 hours getting ready. Suit and hair on point, check. Nerves Together? Hell No.

We arrived at Bailey's house and she emerged. Wow. If ever I Still saw her as a friend, it had just stopped. She looked incredible. I had never really seen her figure before in her baggy t shirts, but her red dress wrapped around her perfectly. Her outfit accessorised with red lip stick and stilettos. She clearly hadn't worn heels much as she walked awkwardly, but I found that cute, endearing even.

She looked so beautiful.

She smiled at me and took my hand. She must have felt me shake as she gripped it tight and kissed me on the cheek, her stilettos allowing her to be almost my height. Mum told her she looked beautiful and gave me a wink, she had definitely caught on that my feelings for Bailey had shifted.

When we got to the school, I still was not scratching. I felt safe with Bailey, proud even to have her on my arm. The kids at school had never seen her look like this, and heads were turning. My nerves had settled as we had a few laughs in the car, Mum leading the conversation. Embarrassing as it was, it was just what I needed.

The dance was in full flow when the DJ decided to introduce the slower music. I could feel myself getting tense. I looked at Bailey and she smiled. She came close and adopted the position that we practiced that night in her room. This time I didn't stand on her toes.

I felt a little heat and started to sweat. Oh no, I thought, here we go. Bailey noticed and pulled her head back. Her dark eyes, again looking into my eyes. She sensed the tension in my body.

She smiled at me. Why is she smiling at me. Then, with a cheeky grin, she stepped on my toe. "Hurts doesn't it," she giggled. Then she leant in, and kissed me.

All the tension seeped out of my body. I didn't need to scratch. I felt warm, but inside. My skin tingled, but with pleasure, with euphoria. I had found my answer. It was my best friend, Bailey.

The Village in the Forest

"I want to turn the clock back to when people lived in small villages and took care of each other"

- Pete Seeger

PROLOGUE

I shivered as I flicked the match and threw it on to the mossy kindling, and watched slowly as orange and violent flames appeared before my eyes. Tonight was cold, every night in our settlement was cold.

I held up my callous and worn palms to the fire, the heat comforting. My weary body allowed itself to drop onto the log underneath me, and I felt the warmth spread through my body, sweat appearing on my brow.

I picked up the stick with the rabbit on it that I had prepared earlier, and placed it in the flames, quietly licking my dry lips as I watched it roast. My stomach quietly rumbled.

The rabbit tasted good, the journey back to our settlement the previous day had left me hungry and tired, but before I rest I must wash. I picked up the wooden bowl, and cleaned the rag as best I could, before brushing it against my face.

I winced as it touched the gruesome burns that now covered my skin.

I looked out at the forest that surrounded me, and all the dark horrors that it contained.

I waited, anxiously, for the decision.

CHAPTER 1

The Forest

I was told when I was just young that the forest surrounds us all, that there is no life outside of it. It's dark and dangerous trees covered the entire earth. My father had warned me never to go outside the boundary of our settlement.

There were other people out there, in the darkness, that much I knew. Occasionally some of our supplies, or even a person, vanished in the night.

Our settlement was small, and was home to maybe six or seven hundred people. We had all lived here all our lives. We were put to work and taught to fight when we turned eight years old - and allowed to stop working once, or should I say if, we reached fifty.

We had fields and plantations around, and families over years had built their own homes out of wood, some in the trees, which I always thought were the most impressive.

I was now in my twenty third year of life, and both my mother and father had reached the age required to retire. My mother, Esme, had taken the offer but still helps out with the young girls, teaching them about things such as child birth and their time of the month. My father, Carlyle, had been the village's only blacksmith, so he carried on his duties. I knew he enjoyed them anyway, the blades he created were his pride and joy - he would never give it up.

He had passed his abilities on to me, and I hoped one day to take over as the head blacksmith when his creaky bones would stop him fulfilling his duty. I spent all my time by his side, picking up all the tricks to forging his great items, and also designing useful things we could use around the settlement.

We were rarely required to use the weapons, apart from to catch animals for food. My father said that we had a few intrusions before I was born - but we needed to be ready if something came. If someone was banished from the settlement, which was also rare, they would be sent out with a sword for protection against whatever lurked deeper in the forest.

The only people allowed into the woods were the fathers, known collectively as rangers, who would be allowed out in groups to find food for their families.

I longed to go into the woods, to see what was out there, but if you leave of your own accord, you are not allowed back - so no one in our town knew what was out there. People preferred to keep it a mystery, but I did not understand that, the more I grew older, the more I sat up in the trees, watching the darkness, conjuring ideas of great adventures.

My time, lately, had been spent with a new woman in my life. We were all encouraged to take a woman, so that the settlement could continue to thrive. We were limited to two children each, otherwise the settlement would become unmanageable - which also meant the pool of potential lovers was limited, but I knew who I wanted, I had always wanted her, she was called Luella.

The village was split into two parts, and whilst it was inhabited by few people it spread far into the forest, long and thin. Luella was born in the area that was in the more dense trees, and the woman were raised differently to the men - so our paths had rarely crossed. With my father being a blacksmith, I lived in one of the clearings, where more people could work with space and freedom.

Every now and again, the village would come together in the clearings for retirement ceremonies, we would dance and drink and celebrate all through the night, and have a day off work. It was on the retirement of a woman named Maida, who was a tailor, that Luella and I got together.

She had looked stunning, her olive skin wrapped in a red dress she had made herself. Her hair, long brown and beautifully braided, flowed down to her waist, with her cheerful face hosting soft red lips and entrancing blue eyes.

We had danced all night, and the other boys had looked on burning with jealousy, whilst the parents had looked on knowing that new love was on the horizon. We had spent the night together - careful not to let our desires get the better of us - we were not supposed to make love until after we were married, due to the child laws.

I knew that I loved Luella, very deeply, and suddenly my desire to explore outside the settlement had vanished. After a few months of courting her, on a beautiful evening up in one of the platforms in the trees, I asked her to be my wife - she giggled, piercing me with those beautiful blue eyes, and said yes.

CHAPTER 2

The Wedding

Weddings were treated with the same level of excitement as our retirement ceremonies, and I knew my marriage to Luella would be no different.

The ceremonies started at mid day, when the sun was at its highest point. The bride and groom would begin in the forest, and walk out into the clearing were they would be wed by the village elders. The elders were a group of retired settlers who decided on the laws of the settlement, and banishment.

After the ceremony, the village would have a big party, with extra food and drink allowed. The bride and groom would sit on a table with their families, up on a platform in the trees that overlooked the clearings - after the food, they would come down and join the rest of the settlers, and dance the night away.

Our wedding had been magical - Luella had looked incredible. Her mother, Freida, and a couple of the other tailors, had designed her a striking white dress that wrapped round her perfect figure, and she wore a small flower headdress, full of colour just like Luella. The village had been buzzing with activity in the lead up, with all the food being prepared, and the tables and flower displays taking over the clearing.

The settlers cheered as we came out of the forest, beaming with happiness, and danced with us through the evening. My mother and father had looked so proud, they were very fond of Luella, and looked forward to the grandchildren we would one day bare them.

In the hours before the wedding, my father had led me out into the trees, and had presented me with a wedding gift. Himself and a couple of the other fathers had built Luella and I our own home, it was perfect, and my mother had decorated it with flowers ready for us to return to after the ceremony.

As the celebrations wound down, and the villagers stumbled home, we did exactly that - and Luella and I made love for the first time, surrounded by flickering candles and beautiful colourful flowers. She dozed off afterwards in my arms, and I contemplated the idea of having my own child, and smiled as I nodded off.

It had been the best day of my life. But everything was about to change.

Luella had woken up early in the morning, her naked body felt amazing in my arms, and we made love again - I was not ready to let go of her soft skin just yet. She rose after that, smiling at me as she put on a dress she had bought with her. She was going to get some water for us to wash - my head was now throbbing with all the drink I had the day before.

As she left our new home, I heard her scream.

I jolted up, tripping over as I dressed myself - my heart thumping with fear, what was happening?

I rushed out of the home, and saw the men holding Luella, with a blade to her throat. I did not recognise them. I was not armed, I was yet to move any of my equipment to my new home, I felt helpless as I looked at her face, which had become sheet white with fear.

The men holding her were dirty, and their clothes ripped and muddy, their faces covered in scars. They were all armed.

I was getting ready to shout for help but I felt my throat tighten as the man holding a sword to Luella's throat put his finger to his sinister grinning mouth.

Our new home was isolated in the trees, a new build on the edge of our village. No one would be able to see us, to help us.

Slowly, the men edged backwards into the trees, I could not chase them as I could not bare to watch them kill the love of my life. I watched her start to cry.

The men disappeared into the dense foliage, and I slapped myself out of my trance. I would follow them, from a distance, see where they were going to take her, and then come back to get help - surely I would not be banished for that, it would be a risk I would have to take. I ran and grabbed some chalk from my home, which my mother had used to write a big 'Welcome Newlyweds,' on the wooden front door.

I held my breathe and crept deeper into the woods behind the men and Luella, who now had a sack on her head and her hands tied. I watched, my blood boiling, as they pushed and shoved her through the trees, laughing every time she fell over. I marked the trees with the chalk as I went, in order to find my way back through this woodland maze.

After what seemed like hours, the men arrived at what looked like a wooden wall, it was tall, and offered their settlement protection, spreading through the trees. Why had we never built anything like this.

I watched as they knocked three times on the front, and then as the door swung open, Luella was pushed inside, and the gate shut sharply behind them. I cursed as I heard more men shouting and laughing, and then turned and ran, as fast as my legs could carry me.

CHAPTER 3

Leaving Home

I arrived back home, empty and alone. My blissfull happiness taken from me. I was angry, I wanted revenge.

The villagers were up and about when I returned, the day after a wedding is a day off, so although most had tried to sleep their hangovers off, I had been gone most of the day, and night was beginning to set in. I needed to find one person - my father, he would know what to do.

I found him up on one of the tree top balconies, he smiled when he saw me, clearly clueless that I had left the village - but the smile quickly vanished when I told him where I had been, and the dreadful events that had transpired that morning.

I started to cry, and he placed his hand on my quivering shoulder. His grip was firm, and I felt it levelling me

"You did the right thing going after her son, don't worry, I will speak to the leaders - they will surely understand. We will find her and get her back to you. For now you must go and rest, I will find you in the morning."

I trudged back to my new home, which was just a shell without the loving embrace of Luella. I did not know how I would rest without my wife. What if last night she became pregnant, and I was to lose my child now as well.

That night I drank all that I had, and sat shivering in the cold - I did not have the energy to make a fire. Slowly the drink took hold of me, and sometime hours later I slipped away into a horrible dream.

"Wake up son, I have spoken to the elders. They are angry, but I have convinced them to allow me and a group of rangers to go out and try and find your wife. You must stay here though, it is forbidden for you to leave. I will follow your chalk marks, I have already been to have a look, they are still there." My father said, standing over me, a grave and unusual look on his usually calm face.

I felt the anger rise inside me, how could they do this? In an instance I hated the village again, furious at the rules. This was my wife, no one else's, it was my revenge, my mission.

As night fell, I watched in frustration as my father and a small group of three hunters prepared their weapons, sharpening their swords, and applying greenery to their clothes, in order to blend in with the forest. The night would give them extra cover.

I secretly did the same, for I would be following them again. Even if it meant I was banished I would not sit by and wait idly.

The chalk would be harder to see at night, so my father had an oil lantern with him - which made him easier to follow. They moved in silence, the only noise the cracks of twigs under their feet and the occasional hoot of an owl.

I could feel my heart pounding I knew we were getting closer. I worried about my sentence when I returned home, if I returned home. I worried for the safety of the people I loved, my father and Luella, my mother would be lost without him, and I would surely be lost without Luella.

I had informed my dad about the knocking procedure I had witnessed when I had watched the men at the gate. As they approached, they blew out their oil lantern.

My father and one of the rangers approached the gate, whilst the other two hid in the bushes near by. Without he lantern, it was difficult to see - I got closer, working my way thought the bushes in complete silence, my fathers hunting training had allowed me to move almost silently.

My father knocked three times, then quickly moved his body flat against the wall. The gate opened, and two men came out. Quickly and efficiently, my father and the ranger took one each, quickly placing their hands on their mouths and dragging them into the bushes.

It was difficult to hear the whole conversation before I heard the disturbing sound of sword entering flesh - but I felt my father had got the information he needed, as I watched himself and the three others crouch and move slowly through the open gate.

Silently, I moved out of the bushes, and grimly glanced at the two corpses lying on the ground. I readied my sword, and slipped through the gate quietly behind them.

CHAPTER 4

The Other Settlement

I found cover quickly, and my father and the other rangers had vanished.

The camp was in a clearing, very similar to ours, with a scattering of wooden buildings built around a centre area, where there was a fire roaring, and a few men sat around it, laughing and drinking. It was late, and I imagine much of the camp had gone to bed.

The camp itself was much smaller than ours, but we did not have time to gather an army to attack these people. We had to rely on the element of surprise

I debated what to do next, frozen in fear. I wondered why these people even took Luella. I saw no women around, so feared the worst, did they need her to grow their population? If they did, we needed to act fast before it came to the worst, if it had not happened already.

I made my way around the back of a few of the buildings, keeping out of sight of the men at the centre of the camp, and it was then that I caught sight of my father. He was making his way quietly to one of the buildings on the far side - it looked bigger than the rest, with double doors rather than single, the fire illuminated a big padlock hanging off the wooden handles. Two men stood out front, one held a make shift torch - a bit of wood with a wick, a flame roaring from the head, the other a sword.

That must be where Luella is, the guards my father interrogated must have confirmed that for him.

I held my breath, my blood cold in my veins, as I watched as my father make it to the back of the building. There were no windows. They would have to get in the front - surely it was impossible, there were too many people, they would definitely be seen.

I tried to get a bit closer, following the route the others had taken, one foot silently placed in front of the other. I got as close as I could when I heard what I had been dreading.

"Intruders, get up everyone, intruders!" Shouted a man running back to the fire. He had gone to relieve himself, and had seen them on the way back.

I watched the horrible events unfold.

My father and the rangers leapt out, cutting down the two people in front of the building with ease, they had not been prepared. More people began shuffling out in shock from the buildings armed and ready to fight. My father was good with his sword, he would need it now.

Three more men went over, cutting down two of our hunters before they were killed by my father and the other ranger.

I watched in horror as the torch the dead man in front of the building had been holding began to catch on the wood housing Luella, the sinister flames licking up quickly around it. I snapped my body out of its frozen state and ran out, stabbing two of the men who did not know I was there.

My father and the other ranger where holding their own valiantly, but the men were coming thick and fast. He had the fact that he was sober and ready to his advantage, as they cut through the men coming at them.

With just a few left, his eyes locked with mine, and they filled with horror. He froze, which gave the enemy the chance they needed, as I watched a sword penetrate through his front.

I screamed as he dropped to his knees, his eyes still fixed on mine, before he slumped to the ground.

I entered an angry daze, I could not believe it. I forgot momentarily about the building burning down in front of me, and charge at the men, driving my sword through them where they stood.

The other hunter saw to the rest, but he was wounded. It

looked bad.

I looked at my fathers still body, and then at the building, the fire now spreading all over it, it was collapsing in, and I could hear screams from within.

I kicked in the door where it stood, it was weakened by the flames, and there she was.

She was still in her dress, but she was sweating, her face terrified. I ran over and embraced her. There were other women with her, all tied up.

"Get out of here," I shouted at her, "Ill get the rest of them, one of ours is outside."

I started untieing some of the others, they were all women, they must have been from other camps. The flames were thicker now, and I could feel my throat tightening, unable to breath in the smoke.

It was then that I felt my clothes set on fire, and the searing heat on my face and the side of my body. The pain was like nothing I had ever felt before.

I freed the last of the women, and managed to roll out of the building. Luella and the hunter had found some water, and threw it on me - the flames extinguishing with a menacing hiss.

I fell down on the blood soaked floor, the adrenaline still pumping, my wife in tears as she slumped down beside me, the surviving ranger tending to my father.

Anyone else in the camp had decided to stay in their homes, and we had no intentions of getting them out. There had been enough death this day.

My face was burnt and scarred, but I still had my life, and my wife.

I crawled over to where my fathers body was lieing. The ranger had covered his wound, and to my relief, it looked like the sword had missed any of his vital parts. He was still breathing, albeit very lightly. My body suddenly filled up with hope, the adrenaline paralysing my own pain. The hunter was hurt too, but not badly.

We looked around the camp, and found a small cart, which we put my father in, between us, we would haul him home, praying for his survival.

I looked at my wife, she was scared, but she was alive. The

love of my life was alive, no burn in the world could take away the happiness I felt at this moment.

EPILOGUE

Luella came over behind me, and kissed me on the cheek, my good cheek. She smiled that beautiful smile, and took the cloth of me, gently pressing it against my cheek. I felt the warmth of her presence all around me, far stronger than the eery presence of the forest.

"The elders of the village have decided to allow you to stay, but you need to work as the blacksmith in your fathers stead. Your father will survive, but he will not be able to work again. The women we saved will be given the option of returning to their own settlements or staying here and helping out other families." She said, kissing me again and hugging me. I winced in pain, but I was not prepared to let her go.

I felt my body relax into her embrace, we had a chance at a life again, and a family.

I looked out at the menacing forest, and for the first time in my life, I hoped I would never had to enter it's terrifying clutches again.

For now, I would enjoy my rabbit, and the company of my beautiful wife. The burns on my face had not quelled my desire for her love.

Writers Block

"When you make a mistake, there are only three things you should ever do about it: admit it, learn from it, and don't repeat it."

- Paul Bear Bryant

THURSDAY, EXAM DAY

I pulled out the chair, it screeched along the wooden floor of the gymnasium. My hands shook as I placed my blue Lamy pen on the table next to the exam paper. My head felt light, my eyelids heavy. The alcohol sweated out of my pores, making my skin itchy.

"You have two hours to complete the paper. You may begin." Said the teacher.

The voice caused my body to tighten. Anxiety. Don't fucking look up.

I opened the paper. I can do this. One exam, write it, get the hell out of here. Get away to university. GET OUT OF THIS TOWN.

Write a story about your greatest achievement. How did it make you feel? How did you overcome the obstacles in the way?

Fuck.

I pushed my crippled little brain as hard as I could. Think, come on, think.

It was no good. The booze clouded my brain, I tried to grab at ideas, but they were quickly pulled back into the mist.

I wiped a bit of sweat out of my brow with my dirty sleeve. I could smell the vodka, practically taste it. I felt watching eyes burning through the side of my head. Don't look. Do not look.

I looked.

Lily's innocent eyes locked with mine. My heart rate increased. Does she know? I forced a smile, it was hardly convincing. My girlfriend smiled back, affectionately. I looked like shit, she must be able to see that.

The guilt made my stomach feel tight. I longed for a drink. I would get one straight after this. But who with.

TUESDAY NIGHT, TWO DAYS BEFORE EXAM

The bar was buzzing with activity, the raucous laughter of the many patrons, the drunken energy bouncing around the room. I should not be here, I should be revising, I should be with Lily. I could not concentrate, not with what I had just done. But I can't concentrate, not tonight. The police had scared the shit out of me. Nobody likes a grass, and now I'm a grass. Another shot, that will help. I stumbled to the bar, the tunnel vision blocking out the euphoria around me.

I muttered my order to the barman. Sambuca. Vodka and Coke. Double. Then I'll go to the toilet, snort a line, maybe two. Yes, I'll feel better after that. My phone vibrated in my pocket. Even that gave me anxiety, made my heart pump more and more. A text from Lily. I'll speak to her tomorrow. Eight missed calls from Bea, what was that about? I downed the shot, as I turned away I jumped as a hand grabbed my jacket. Everything was making me flinch. A soft voice whispered playfully in my ear, I recognised it instantly.

"Well hello there. You should be at home revising. But since you're here, you can buy me a drink."

THURSDAY, EXAM DAY

The flashback put me more on edge. No, it was pushing me over the edge. My whole body was vibrating now. I wished I could just empty my mind, but it was going at a hundred miles an hour.

I looked again, Lily had carried on writing. Suddenly I felt jealous. Lily would smash this exam, she was smart, beautiful and sensible. What the fuck was she doing with me. I would have to tell her, I could not live with this guilt. I have to break up with her. I need to pass this exam, get away. Stop fucking looking at her you idiot, it's only going to make you feel worse.

Don't look straight either. What is in front is even worse.

Tick. Tick. Tick. Fuck. The clock. The exam. I picked up the pen, struggling to grip it with my clammy, sweaty fingers. They wanted to be around a glass, not a pen. Anything to get rid of this feeling. I tried to push my brain again, what had I ever actually fucking achieved?

I'm eighteen, I have a girlfriend who knows nothing about me, I've drunk every day since I was sixteen, I do loads of drugs, I hate sports, I am unemployed. Oh, and don't forget, my mum now thinks I am a criminal, and if I don't pass this exam, they are going to kick me out. Hell yea, I'm an achiever alright. Shit.

Tick, Tick, Tick. I need to get something down. Think you useless prick. You like writing, there must be something.

TUESDAY AFTERNOON - 2 DAYS BEFORE EXAM

My mum's voice roared up the stairs. "Get down here boy, the police are here, they want to speak to you, what the hell have you been up to."

Fuck. Fuck. Fuck. I leapt up, my heart racing. I sealed the big bag of white powder, and wrapped it up in a ball of old t shirts. I threw it under the bed, as well as the half empty bottle of vodka. I still had a line on the Bad Boys DVD case on my desk. It would help. I rolled up a tenner. The hit was instant, suddenly I was ready. I could talk my way out of this, they did not need to know anything. Stop sweating, pull yourself together.

The policeman was sat on the sofa, my mother had made him a coffee. Hopefully her kindness will butter him up. Fat chance. He eyed me up, and down, and up again. I looked like shit, skinny and pale, and probably stank of booze.

He started talking, but his words were not going in. I was so high, in a daze. He wanted to know about Mikey. Mikey from Bream Street. He had seen me going in and out of his house. They had officers outside, they had been watching him. But he had disappeared.

I knew exactly where he was. The policeman struck fear into my heart. He was big, stocky, he spoke directly and firmly. His face told a thousand stories, he had seen action, he was not here to be messed around. He threatened to search my room and the house, unless I gave him information. He would definitely find my stash. I would be arrested, kicked out of the house and out of school.

I had to tell him, I had no choice.

When the policeman left the anxiety completely took hold of me.

I ignored my mum. She wanted answers to. She can fuck off. I went upstairs, drank the rest of the vodka. Snorted another line. I needed to go. Where should I go. I can't see Lily. The bar, I will go to the bar.

THURSDAY, EXAM DAY

The quiet scratching of pens and rustling of papers bought me back to reality. This cold, dark reality. I needed a drink. What sort an eighteen year old *needs* a drink, I'm such a loser.

I looked at the blank paper in front of me, irritated by the organised lines on the A4 page. I wished my life could be as organised as this piece of paper.

All I could think about now was Mikey from Bream Street. I owed him money for my last visit, and now I had fucking grassed on him. He would beat the crap out of me if he found out. I hoped the police had found him, locked him up, then I would be safe.

His little brother, Greg from Bream Street, sat four rows to my right. I allowed myself to look at him. His eyes were red rimmed, his hair messy and dirty. He looked rough as well. He loved his brother, but stayed out of his activities. The police must have been harassing them. It was my association with his brother that had ruined our friendship. If I had told the police I had been round to see Greg, Greg would have told them it was a lie - and probably know straight away that it was me that grassed up his brother.

His presence made me nervous. I felt like I was in a cauldron, a hot pot of anxiety. Look left, I see my girlfriend, who's heart I was about to break. Look right, I see Greg, who's brother was going to go to prison because of me, look straight, and I see *her.*

My mind once again digressed from the task at hand. So many things were on my mind now, bouncing around, each thought adding to the tension in my body. I craved a drink, it would make this go away, maybe I would be able to do the exam.

Tick, Tick, Tick.

"What is it," the teacher said, but not to me. The voice again crippling me with every syllable. That voice, that playful voice.

"Please can I go to the loo." Replied the student behind me. I looked around. It was Bea. My best friend Bea. Some friend I had been to her. We used to hang out all the time, but lately drugs and alcohol had taken her spot. She worried about me, I knew that. It's probably the reason I avoid her at the moment. She knew me better than anyone, and I felt ashamed around her.

As she walked past me, she locked eyes with me. She looked angry, really angry. Wait, was I meant to have done something with her. Think, think, did she called me last week, did she want me to do something?

Oh Fuck

THURSDAY NIGHT, WEEK BEFORE EXAM

As I took another shot, I looked out of my bedroom window. The world seemed blurry, my head was spinning. Shit. I needed to pee, but I didn't want to risk seeing my mum. I needed to go round Mikey's, get a fresh batch. I was running low. I couldn't go tonight, I could barely stand. It's pretty sad that I am just spending my nights getting drunk alone.

My phone buzzed, it was probably Lily. She was getting pretty sick of me lately, I never saw her, and when I did I was hungover or high. It wasn't Lily. I squinted at the screen. Bea?

I answered. She knew I was drunk straight away. She wanted to come and make sure I was ok. I told her not too.

"Look man, you are like a brother to me. I know your Dad's death hit you hard. We all miss him, but you've totally lost yourself. You're going to fuck your life up. Please talk to me. Your a smart guy, and I love you."

I took her words in, they were all true. I missed my Dad like crazy, and the drinking had all started when he died. Those dark days had become dark weeks, and then dark months. Joints turned to alcohol, alcohol turned to cocaine. I tried to talk, but words wouldn't come out. Bea carried on talking.

"Look, the reason I'm ringing is because I really need a favour. I wouldn't ask if I didn't really need it. My parents are out of town next week. I have a job interview on Tuesday night - it's really important and I can't find anyone to look after my little brother. Can you do it, please?"

I said yes. Of course I could help my best friend, she had always been there for me. Perhaps I should write it down, i'm so wasted what if I don't remember. No, of course I will remember. I would never let Bea down.

THURSDAY, EXAM DAY

My heart sank as I remembered. I had let down my best friend, the one person who I had promised myself I would never let down. I had never felt so low, so mentally destroyed. Everyone around me hated me apart from Lily, but I could not even look her in the eyes, not after what I did. What I did when I was supposed to be helping Bea. What I did when I was supposed to be revising.

I watched as Bea walked back in, she passed my desk this time without even looking at me. I felt so ashamed, the anxiety now totally overwhelming. I needed to talk to her afterwards. But could I deal with that, without going totally mad? I already was mad. Alcohol and it's little white friend had now totally torn my life apart.

I looked back over at Lily, and then Greg, they were both scribbling away, creating a future for themselves. I was just sat here, thinking about how I had personally destroyed mine. I needed to write something. Fuck, I needed to get out of this room, it was strangling me, suffocating me.

"That's one hour gone, you have one hour left," said the teacher. The voice sending shivers down my spine, and flashbacks once again crashed around my head.

This time, I could not help but look up.

WEDNESDAY MORNING, DAY BEFORE EXAM

My head was pounding, I felt like a bomb had gone off in it. I opened my eyes, and the sun shining in through the window instantly stung. My brain tried to gather itself, and I realised I had no idea where I was, the soft sheets felt strange, where was I. I looked over at the bedside table - on it was my phone, the screen smashed. Fuck. I tried to turn it on, nothing. Lily is going to be pissed.

"Morning gorgeous."

I froze, I recognised that voice. Was that….

Surely not

I felt a warm arm wrap around my body, and soft lips gently kissed my neck. It definitely was not Lily. What had I done now! I held my breathe, and turned over.

Fuck

It was Miss Grayson. My English teacher. What the hell.

I flashed back to last night, the bar. The woman who whispered in my ear. Then it all came flooding back. The woman with the playful voice had been Miss Grayson. Each memory bringing fresh feelings of shock. We had stayed at the bar till close, she had taken me back to her place. I thought about the policeman in the afternoon. My life was well and truly in the gutter, and now I have gone and slept with my teacher?

She had to go, she had to go and teach a class at school, my fucking school! My mind exploded. I needed a drink. I went to the shop, bought a bottle. I had promised that I would not tell anyone - not that I wanted to. But it's the last thing I needed on my conscience.

I got home and put my phone on charge, it lit up through the crack

227

in the screen. Thank god. Mum was out at work. Thank god.

I saw all the missed calls - Lily, Bea (what did she want?!), My mum. There was couple from a number I did not recognise as well, could that be Mikey - what if he knew.

It was all too much, way too much. I cracked open the vodka, it soothed me.

THURSDAY, EXAM DAY.

Miss Grayson sat at the end of the exam hall, and her presence was destroying me. I was sat in a room with my girlfriend, and the woman who I had cheated on her with. The woman that was also my fucking teacher.

She saw me gazing at her, and gave me a playful smirk, I could practically feel her hands all over my body, it made me shudder. It did nothing but make me feel ready to detonate. I looked at Lily, scribbling away. Her pen moving efficiently and effortlessly. Blissfully unaware of the chaos going on in my head right now.

I thought about getting up and leaving, my life was just a total train wreck.

This exam was my only way out of this mess. I could do this exam. I had an idea.

Everyone was probably writing some bullshit about their work on the sports field, or a job they got, or something like that. Hell, my greatest achievement was just making it to this exam! I have put myself in a room claustrophobically full of agony, everywhere I look is a trigger for something terrible that I have done. Yet I am here. I battled through my hangover to get here, I did my other exams. I can do this, I can deal with the rest later.

Was this a ridiculous idea. I couldn't think about anything else. My journey to this exam hall had generated some of the strongest and scariest feelings I had ever experienced, why not write about them. It will definitely stand out if nothing else. Fuck it. What other choice do I have.

I looked around one last time, I had just under an hour to do this. I had a plan. It had helped settle me down, perhaps writing it all out would make me feel better. I know I could smoothe things over with Bea. Lily would dump me, but she would be off to university soon anyways. Mikey surely is going to jail, and how would anyone find out it was me that grassed him up. I felt the alcohol cloud temporarily lift.

Just whatever you do, do not look at the teacher. She was just sat there, like a totem pole of my stupidity. She haunted the exam room, and she would now haunt my thoughts for a long time to come.

Don't look at the teacher.

I started to write.

Tick, Tick, Tick.

FRIDAY, TWO MONTHS AFTER THE EXAM

I pushed open the double doors, my suitcase wheeling noisily behind me. I breathed in the fresh air - my mind clear.

Bea stood outside, leaning on her navy blue Corsa. She smiled at me, and then came over and hugged me, it felt good.

I turned around and looked back at the building that had been my home for nearly two months. I had checked in shortly after the exam, after I had told Lily that I had cheated on her. I had never told her who with. It didn't matter. She said she was going to break up with my anyway, but in all honesty it felt good to tell her the truth (sort of). I missed her, but the booze had never really allowed me to fully love her. She always came second. I wanted to meet someone now who would come first.

Bea had accepted my apology, and she had helped me get a place at rehab, and then pretty much dragged me there. She was a good girl.

I had been alcohol free for nearly two months, the crippling anxiety was now under control. Mikey had also gone down, and his family had moved away - there was no chance anyone would know that it had been me that grassed. It also came out that he had been responsible for a number of more violent crimes, which I had not known about, so I did not feel so bad about telling the police where he was.

We drove for a while, Bea chatted away about everything that had been going on, her voice was soothing, I welcomed it.

She said Miss Grayson had been fired, apparently she had

been sleeping with students. Bea thought it was crazy. I went along with it. Bea looked at me, and raised an eyebrow. No more was said about it,

"Hey, your mum and I opened your exam results. We thought we would wait to tell you on the outside.

"You did really well man, all things considered, but your English Exam - you got an A*, one of the top grades in the country apparently. You got into your university as well, was it Plymouth?"

"Just out of interest, the question in the English language exam, your greatest achievement, what did you write about?"

ACKNOWLEDGMENTS

It's been one hell of a journey getting to the place where this book can be in your hands. It's certainly not been an easy one, but to realise a life long dream of seeing my name in print is truly something special. There is no way I could possibly even list all the people that have helped me along the way, I am so blessed with a truly remarkable number of people around me. I'll have a crack as best as I can though.

First of all I want to thank my family, my mother - Dee, for always nagging (sorry encouraging) me to actually start writing. To my brother Tizi, and his lovely wife Sophie, and their two wonderful children, Hector and Valentine. They put up with me whilst I wrote the bulk of my work, and also kept me fed and relatively sane! Also I want to mention my Dad - Sebastion. Sadly, he is no longer with us, but he had a huge influence on my life, and writing the speech for the celebration of his life was one experience that made me think I could actually do this.

A lot of the stories in this book are about addiction, which is something that I struggled with a lot before I wrote this book, and probably will have to deal with my whole life. It led to me having to go away for a little while to sort myself out, and this leads to anxiety and isolation, which is something a lot of my characters struggle with. I want to give a big shout to all the staff at the clinic I went to for helping through the hardest period of my life, you helped me learn so much about myself which I was able to channel into this book. To come through that, and truly feel yourself again, you need some amazing people around you. Throughout my struggles with alcohol I was supported massively by my best friend Declan. I honestly can't imagine my life without him, he is not even my rock, he is my boulder. Also to his girlfriend Chloe, and also my friend Rich. I couldn't have decided to throw the bottle away without them, and therefore there would have been no book.

Of course, since then, once I started writing, there were so many amazing friends around me. Amy, James, Nat, Blob, Sarah, Meg, Sam, Leng, Elliot, Luke, Matt, Luker, Cam, Daisy, Lex, Han and Nick - you guys are all awesome and I couldn't have done this without you. Furthermore, my housemate Tom, who just about puts up with me most of the time, and occasionally laughs at me when I'm at my best. You have some serious patience! Thanks also goes to a best friend and fellow writer Jess as well, she always pushed me to be the best that I can be.

I also want to mention the best chef in the west, Tom, who owned the local pub and kept me fed and entertained throughout my writing. His housemate Jack was always there to keep me busy in the daytime when everyone else was busy at work.

I also want to thank the Liam's, Colleen, Nathan, Cyrus, and Adam. You guys have been awesome. Daniel as well, perhaps I might give you that first edition you wanted.

Thanks to Brandon Novak as well, your book 'Dreamseller,' was one of the most inspirational things I have ever read.

There is so many more people to talk about that have had an impact on my life and helped me to be able to write these stories, but it's impossible to list them all, so I just want to say thank you to pretty much everyone! Your all amazing, and I hope you enjoy my stories. This is not the end...

Printed in Great Britain
by Amazon